MEASLE
AND THE
WRATHMONK

Other books in the series

MEASLE AND THE DRAGODON
MEASLE AND THE MALLOCKEE

MeaSLe
AND THE
WRaTHMONK

Ian Ogilvy

Illustrated by Chris Mould

OXFORD
UNIVERSITY PRESS

For Barnaby and Matilda

OXFORD
UNIVERSITY PRESS

Great Clarendon Street, Oxford OX2 6DP

Oxford University Press is a department of the University of Oxford.
It furthers the University's objective of excellence in research, scholarship,
and education by publishing worldwide in

Oxford   New York

Auckland   Cape Town   Dar es Salaam   Hong Kong   Karachi
Kuala Lumpur   Madrid   Melbourne   Mexico City   Nairobi
New Delhi   Shanghai   Taipei   Toronto

With offices in

Argentina   Austria   Brazil   Chile   Czech Republic   France   Greece
Guatemala   Hungary   Italy   Japan   Poland   Portugal   Singapore
South Korea   Switzerland   Thailand   Turkey   Ukraine   Vietnam

Oxford is a registered trade mark of Oxford University Press
in the UK and in certain other countries

British Library Cataloguing in Publication Data

Data available

ISBN-13: 978-0-19-275516-2
ISBN-10: 0-19-275516-1

1 3 5 7 9 10 8 6 4 2

Printed by Cox & Wyman,
Reading, Berkshire

CONTENTS

A HORRIBLE HOUSE

Measle Stubbs was ten and a half years old. He was small, thin, and bony. Most of the time, he was as hungry as a very hungry horse. He had a short snub nose, high cheekbones, a pair of eyes coloured a deep, emerald green, and (when he felt like it) a wide and friendly smile. His hair was brown and stood up all over his head in spiky tufts. It was the oddest haircut—long where it should have been short, short where it should have been long—and the reason it was like this was because Measle cut his hair himself, using a blunt and rusty kitchen knife, with which he sawed and hacked at his hair whenever it got so long that it fell in his eyes. Apart from being the most uneven haircut imaginable, it also hadn't been washed in a very long time. Neither had his clothes and sometimes he smelt pretty bad, particularly when the weather was warm. It wasn't warm very often where Measle Stubbs lived. Measle Stubbs lived in a cold and horrible house. It was not Measle's choice to live there; it was *circumstances*.

The horrible house was at the far end of a dreary, dirty street full of dirty, dreary houses—but three things set this house apart from all the others. The first was the way it looked—all black, with a tall, pointed roof, tall dark narrow windows like blind eyes, and tall, soot-caked chimneys that looked like dirty fingers pointing at the sky. The other houses in the street just looked dingy and dreary but Measle's house looked as if something bad had happened in it—and, quite possibly, something bad could happen there again tomorrow.

The second fact that made it different from the other houses in the street was that it was the only one that was occupied. All the other houses had been deserted by their owners a long time ago and their doors and windows boarded over. If you stood at the far end of the street and looked down its length, you'd have thought that every house there was abandoned and derelict. But if you looked a little harder, you might have seen—down at the far end of the street—a faint glimmer of light from an attic window, which was the only indication that there was anybody living in the street at all.

The third fact that made the house different from all the others was also the strangest: all day and all night, winter, summer, autumn, and spring, there was a small, black cloud that hung, never moving, over the dismal roof, dribbling a steady, constant stream of rain that fell only on the house where Measle Stubbs lived and not at all on any of the others in the street.

The house belonged to Basil Tramplebone and Basil Tramplebone was Measle Stubbs's Legal Guardian. Measle lived in the house with just his Legal Guardian for company—and his Legal Guardian wasn't good company at all; in fact, his Legal Guardian hardly spoke because he hated everybody—but that was all right because everybody who had ever met him hated Basil Tramplebone. He was very tall and thin and he always wore black clothes. A black coat and a black shirt and a black tie; black trousers and black socks and black shoes. His greasy hair was black and he parted it in the middle and

3

plastered it down on his head with black shoe polish. The only things that weren't black about him were his face and his hands: Basil's face was very white, as though all the blood had been drained out and replaced with milk. His eyes were like fish eyes—staring and blank and very, very cold. His long, bony hands were the colour of candles and the skin was so dry that it rustled when he rubbed his palms together, which he did when he was pleased. Basil Tramplebone wasn't pleased very often, so the rustling noise didn't happen very often.

If the outside of Basil Tramplebone's house was grim and gloomy and depressingly ugly, the inside was even worse. It was so ghastly that Measle only dared go into three rooms—the kitchen, the bathroom, and the attic. All the rooms in the house smelt bad—each one in a different way—but at least being in the kitchen and the bathroom and the attic didn't frighten him half to death. He certainly didn't dare go into the room that was supposed to be his bedroom. There was a huge black oak wardrobe in there, full of clothes that weren't his. They felt damp and smelt of mildew. Once, Measle had got up enough courage to sort through the clothes. He stopped doing that when he found the jacket. It was made of some sort of rough material and it had *three* sleeves—two in the usual places and a third that stuck out at the back. When he finally got up the courage to ask

Basil about it, Basil told him to mind his own business—but if he *must* know, then all the clothes in the wardrobe had been left there, over the years, by visiting friends of his, some of whom were, perhaps, a little *different*.

The wardrobe was in one dark corner of the room and a great, black bed that looked like a coffin was in the other. There were black velvet curtains over the windows and the glass in the windows was painted black, so you couldn't see out at all and, what with the black painted walls and ceiling and floorboards, it was one of the gloomiest rooms you can imagine and one that would certainly give you nightmares if you tried to sleep in it—so Measle didn't try at all. Instead, he slept on a pile of old rags in the kitchen, right up by the ancient iron stove, which was the only place in that dreadful house that was warm.

Measle hated Basil Tramplebone and, of course, Basil Tramplebone hated Measle, because Basil Tramplebone hated everybody. He only looked after Measle because Measle's mother and father had been killed by an encounter with a deadly snake when Measle was four years old, leaving poor little Measle an orphan.

The story about the deadly snake had come from Basil who, in Measle's experience, always told the truth. But in this case, Measle wasn't so sure—

perhaps because he badly wanted his parents to be alive. So, deep in his heart, Measle was certain that his mother and father were still around somewhere and that, one day, they would come back to him. Meanwhile, his parents had left a lot of money in the bank and now it was all Measle's —but a judge had said that Measle was too young to have control of all that money and too young to live by himself and had appointed Basil—who said he was Measle Stubbs's fourth cousin twelve times removed and, therefore, Measle's closest living relative—to look after him and his money. The odd thing was, (although Measle had been too young to remember this now) the judge had looked a little like Basil. The same black clothes, the same cold, fishy eyes, the same white, white face. He'd even talked a bit like Basil too—and, every time he'd looked at Basil, he'd smiled like a crocodile—as if he was approving of everything that Basil said.

Of the three rooms that Measle could bear to be in, the attic was his favourite. The bathroom smelt bad and the water that came out of the taps was brown, with green, floating bits in it, so Measle didn't bath very often. At least there was a window in the bathroom and, sometimes, Measle would stand on the cracked lavatory seat and look out of the window at the dismal railway yards that were behind the house and dream of living somewhere else.

The kitchen was warm and dry but it smelt of rotten cabbages and was infested with enormous cockroaches. Some of them were so big that, when Measle stepped on them, they didn't go *crunch* under his foot like the smaller ones did—they simply wriggled about in a disgusting way until Measle took his foot off them and then they scuttled away under the stove, quite unharmed.

As far as the attic was concerned, Measle had only recently discovered it, because Basil had never allowed him to go up there before. *Something* interesting had certainly been going on up that narrow flight of stairs, because Basil spent many hours in the attic and for a long time Measle used to stand at the bottom of the stairs and listen —and, occasionally, he'd heard sounds that he couldn't explain to himself. And then, one day, about six months earlier, Basil had said, 'Come with me, Measle,' and then he'd led the way up the cramped, steep staircase and into the extraordinary attic room—and Measle's jaw had dropped in amazement at what he saw.

It was the biggest—and probably the best— miniature railway set in the world.

From that moment, the attic became the one room in the house that Measle actually didn't mind spending time in. It was still a scary room—there was something in there that lived up in the rafters. Measle had seen movement up there among the dark beams of wood and, once, a pair of red, glowing eyes. What the something was, Measle didn't really want to know—just so long as the something stayed up there out of sight and never put in an appearance. At least there were no cockroaches in the attic—in fact, there were no insects of any kind up there, which was odd because the rest of the house was crawling with them.

Measle was fascinated by the train set. Somehow, Basil Tramplebone had managed to build a miniature version of the dismal railway yards on a huge table, right in the middle of the attic. The table was so big that there was only a narrow gap all the way round between the edge of the table and the attic walls and it was a good thing that both Measle and Basil were so thin, otherwise they could never have fitted in the narrow space. Everything on the enormous table was accurate, down to the smallest detail—the coal yard had a mound of tiny chips of real coal, the street lights shone with a sickly yellow light, and there was a constant, tiny stream of dirty water flowing in the miniature gutters—but further out, away from the town, Basil had changed the look. Instead of rows and rows of cheap, sooty houses (which Measle could see beyond the railway lines if he looked out of the bathroom window) Basil had created a forest of tall pines, with the trees set so close together it was hard to see between them. It was very dark and gloomy, with strange little houses here and there in clearings in the woods. The houses were quite different from the grimy houses round the railway yards. They were made of little logs, with stone chimneys and porches on the front and Measle decided that, if he was an inhabitant of the place, he'd much rather live in one of them than in the depressing town.

When Basil played with his train set—and if he was in a good mood—he would let Measle come up to the attic to watch. From the very start of being allowed to watch Basil play with his trains, it was obvious to Measle that Basil didn't care for anything modern. There were no electric commuter trains, no long-distance diesel trains. Everything about the set was old-fashioned and all the locomotives were steam engines from an age gone past. There were two sorts of trains— passenger trains and freight trains—and each one was detailed to the smallest degree. When Measle sat on a chair and watched, he would stay very quiet and still (because Basil Tramplebone hated noise and fidgeting), and he would look down at the layout and, every time he did so, he saw something new in the scenery and that's what he liked best about coming up to the attic and watching Basil play with his trains.

One day, he saw that Basil had made a little plume of smoke to come from the chimney of one of the cabins in the woods; another time, Basil had built a water tower by the side of the tracks and, when one of the freight trains stopped underneath it, the tower let out a tiny trickle of water that filled the boiler of the engine. Once, Measle noticed that Basil had added a lake in the middle of the forest—not with real water this time, which was a disappointment, but with a mirror embedded in the surface, surrounded by the little pine trees. It looked realistic enough, and the way the mirror reflected the dark pine trees and the rocks of the shoreline was probably more effective than if the lake had been made with real water. Measle had to admit that Basil was good with his hands. It seemed as though Basil could make just about anything, so long as the thing was very small. Sometimes Measle was amazed at the details of all the scaled-down objects—every window in the houses looked like real glass, every leaf on the trees looked as if it would certainly drop off when autumn came round and every worn paving stone on the dirty pavements looked as if it had been trodden on by countless shuffling feet.

There were quite a few people in the model too. The painted plastic figures were positioned about the train set, doing all the things that people usually do—shopping, gossiping on street corners, standing on station platforms waiting for trains. There were a few animals as well—a little black and white dog sniffing round a lamp-post, a cat lounging on a windowsill and, deep in the forest, a family of three black bears walking in a line near the lake.

When Basil Tramplebone played with his trains, he always ate a whole box of glazed doughnuts and drank a gallon of pink lemonade out of a plastic jug—and some of the crumbs and some of the sugar and an occasional drop of lemonade would fall onto the table top. He kept the box and the jug close by his side. Measle never got a doughnut or a glass of lemonade because Basil never offered him any and Measle didn't dare ask. Measle would stare at the crumbs, hoping that Basil would perhaps want to go to the lavatory and then, while he was gone, Measle could sneak over and lick his finger and dab up the crumbs and the sugar and eat them—but Basil never seemed to go to the lavatory at all, even after eating a whole box of glazed doughnuts and drinking a gallon of pink lemonade, so Measle never got the chance.

Measle Stubbs missed his mother and father badly. He couldn't remember what they looked like, because their unfortunate encounter with the snake had happened when he was very young but, all the same, he wished it was them who were looking after him and not Basil Tramplebone. Basil Tramplebone didn't like looking after anything or anybody—apart from himself and his train set, of course. He looked after himself and his train set very well indeed. He fed himself the best steaks and gave Measle the fat from round the edges. He always made chips for himself but plain boiled potatoes for Measle—and sometimes they weren't cooked all the way through and were hard in the middle. Basil Tramplebone's black socks were made of silk and so were his black boxer shorts; Measle didn't have any socks and only two pairs of underpants and the elastic had stopped working in both of them. But it was the train set that Basil cared for the most and he spent hours and hours and hours working on it and tons and tons and tons of Measle's money on the most expensive equipment he could buy.

Measle didn't mind so much about the money spent on the train set because the train set was probably the best in the world and he liked looking at it. On the other hand, he didn't like Basil spending all that money on silk socks and silk boxer shorts, when all he had were two pairs of underpants with broken elastic—and he *certainly* didn't like Basil buying the best steaks and chips with Stubbs money and then not letting him have any. Measle thought that was totally unfair.

One night, while he lay curled tight up against the stove, an idea came to him. He hadn't been able to get to sleep because the cockroaches were having a party—or what sounded like a party if cockroaches had them—under the stove. There was a lot of clicking and rustling and tap-tap-tapping of cockroach feet and he couldn't sleep with all that noise going on, so he decided to think instead. That was when the idea came to him. It was a brilliant idea. It was, he admitted to himself, also a dangerous idea but the best ideas often are and Measle was prepared to take the risk.

The next day, at lunch (Basil was having fried sausages and bacon and chips and ketchup and Measle was having a piece of stale bread and a paper cup of water) Measle said, 'Oh, Mr Tramplebone, sir, the bank called this morning. They want to see you.'

'The bank?' said Basil. He stared at Measle with his fish eyes. 'When?'

'While you were still asleep, sir,' said Measle, who was good at lying. 'Something about some extra money.'

'Money?'

'Yes. To us, of course. They want to see you about it. The man said something about investing it.'

'Invesssting?' Basil always hissed like a rattlesnake whenever he said the letter S.

'Yes, Mr Tramplebone. He said it was too much just to leave in an ordinary bank account.'

'Too much?'

'Yes.'

'I shall telephone them.'

'Yes, sir—but the trouble is, the telephone doesn't seem to be working any more, sir.'

'Not working?'

'No, sir.'

The reason the telephone wasn't working any more was because Measle had taken the plug out of the socket. He watched nervously as Basil tried the phone. Basil listened to the earpiece for a moment and then hissed like a snake.

'What a nuisssance.' He put the receiver down. Then, he put on his long black coat and picked up his long black umbrella, which looked like a sleeping vampire bat.

'I'm going out, Measle,' he hissed. 'To the bank. Behave yoursssself. Do nothing. Nothing at all.'

Basil hardly ever went out. He had all their food delivered from the local supermarket and bought all his clothes and stuff for the train set from catalogues, so he never needed to leave the house at all. In fact, when the door closed behind him, Measle realized that this was the first time he could remember ever being alone in the house and, for a moment, he felt scared. Then he said to himself, 'What can a house do to you? It's not like it's a burglar or a murderer or a mugger or anything, so what can it possibly do to you?' That made him feel a little better, but not a lot.

He looked through a crack in the front door and watched Basil stride down the path to the street. A small piece of the black cloud that hung over the house detached itself and began to follow Basil. It dribbled a little shower of rain on Basil's open umbrella. At the end of the path, Basil turned right, which was the way to the better part of town, where the bank was. Basil was going to have to walk the whole way, because they didn't have a car and there were no buses that came out to this side of the railway yards. The bank was about a mile and a half away, which meant that Basil was going to have to walk three miles and, even with his long, spider legs, that was going to take some time.

It was enough time, thought Measle. More than enough time.

The Train Set

Measle's brilliant idea was this: once he'd got Basil Tramplebone out of the house, he would climb up the stairs to the attic and push open the door and sit down on Basil Tramplebone's special high stool and reach over and turn the master knob—the one that brought the train set to life—and then, well, he'd just sit there and play with the biggest and probably best train set in the entire world for an hour or so.

Of course, Measle's idea wasn't really all that brilliant. Basil Tramplebone would get to the bank and find out that there wasn't any extra money at all—and then he'd find out about the telephone—and that would make him completely furious and when Basil Tramplebone was completely furious,

Measle's life became even nastier than before. But Measle didn't think of this, because he was so excited by the rest of the plan. The idea of playing with Basil's train set without any interference was just too good to pass up.

Something else that was too good to pass up was the opportunity to eat something. Measle went quickly to the kitchen—it smelt even worse than usual today—and opened the ancient refrigerator. He was hoping to find something nice in there but there was nothing at all, except a paper bag full of old, wrinkled carrots down at the bottom, in the vegetable tray. Measle didn't particularly like carrots but he hadn't had one for such a long time that he'd forgotten what they tasted like, so he stuffed the paper bag into his pocket and then headed for the staircase.

Measle raced up the creaking stairs, flight after flight, until he arrived, panting for breath, right at the top of the house. The attic door stood open. Measle went in and stared at the huge table. He carefully avoided looking up towards the rafters.

It had been a month since he was last in here; was there anything new—anything that hadn't been there before? He looked all over the enormous table—yes, there were some changes. Not with the set itself—the tracks and the trains were all in their usual places and none of the buildings had been altered. But Basil had moved some of the model people around and he'd put several of them into some very odd situations. There, for instance, near the coal yards—a workman in a blue coat and a yellow plastic helmet was sitting on the edge of a rectangular hole in the pavement, his hands full of what appeared to be electrical cables. Obviously Basil wanted it to look as if the man was making repairs to the mains power supply. But that wasn't all Basil wanted to show, for standing directly behind this workman—and unseen by him—was another figure of a man holding a bucket of water high in the air—and Measle saw that the bucket of water was about to be tipped over the workman!

Measle knew that water and electricity was a very dangerous combination.

Measle frowned. This was very odd. He looked over the train set again. What else was different? Ah—there, deep in the woods—the trio of bears were no longer strolling by the mirror lake. Now they were clustered round the base of a pine tree and all staring hungrily upwards—and there, high in the branches, was the figure of a little girl, dressed as a Brownie, clinging tightly to the tree trunk! Measle looked further—his eyes stopping on the scene that was taking place in a siding near one of the stations. A group of people were bending over something on the railway tracks. He looked closer. The something was an old woman —and the people clustered around her were tying her down on the rails!

This is weird, thought Measle. Why had Basil decided that some of the townspeople should be threatened like this? He started searching the train set again. There—in the town square, at the foot of the Town Hall steps—a figure of a woman, crouching in obvious terror, her fists pressed tightly over her eyes so as to block out the sight of the huge Bengal tiger that was creeping steadily towards her!

Measle grinned. He couldn't help it. There was something quite funny about all this. These poor people, all in such danger—but not really in any danger at all, of course, since everything was just plastic and nothing was real—other than Basil's strange imagination. Well, he'd certainly made the train set even more fascinating than ever. Was there anything else to see? Oh yes, there—a round, fat little man with a shiny bald head, carrying what looked like a heavy suitcase, running as fast as his short legs could carry him down a street that led out towards the forest. Behind him, in close pursuit, was a small mob of people, carrying banners and placards on sticks. Measle leaned closer, peering at the tiny writing on the placards. 'DOWN WITH KNOWLEDGE!' was written on one and 'DEATH TO A SALESMAN!' was on another.

Weirder and weirder, thought Measle.

Anything else? He'd covered the town pretty closely—what about the forest? Anything other than the Brownie and the bears? Oh yes! There in

Signs read:
DOWN WITH KNOWLEDGE
DEATH TO A SALESMAN
DOWN WITH SALESMEN
NO TO KNOWLE[DGE]

a clearing of cut down trees. A big black man was sitting on a tree stump. At his feet lay a canvas tool bag and next to it, a tiny chainsaw and a red fuel can. The man's broad shoulders were slumped and his head hung low. There was a look of despair about him and he seemed oblivious to the three figures creeping up behind him. The figures were modelled and painted to look like lumberjacks. They were approaching him with great stealth and all three were carrying axes raised over their heads.

For a moment, Measle wondered whether it might be fun to rescue all these poor people from their predicaments. He could put the bears back by the lake, he could throw the Bengal tiger out of the attic window, he could untie the ropes that bound the old woman to the railway tracks—but no, that would be really stupid. Basil would get horribly angry if he messed about with the layout. What he was about to do was bad enough but perhaps he might get away with it just this once— but if he changed anything that Basil had set up so carefully, then Basil would be sure to notice and then he'd be in real trouble. Having made the decision, he squeezed through the narrow gap between the edge of the table and the wall, until he came to the Control Box.

The Control Box didn't look like the usual sort of electric train console; for a start, there weren't any plastic parts to it. The whole thing was made of black metal and all the knobs were black metal too and the knobs were larger than usual and had strange markings on them—but Measle had never seen an ordinary train controller, so he didn't think this one was odd at all.

There was a tall stool where Basil Tramplebone sat. Measle climbed up onto it. If he leaned forward he could just about reach all the knobs. He knew which one started up the power and which ones controlled the different sections of track, because he'd watched Basil carefully for a long time, so he reached out and turned the big black knob on the left of the control panel and there was a low hum as the power came on. So far, so good. Now, which train to start with?

The train Measle liked best was a little green freight train with a tall smokestack and two flatbed trucks that it pulled behind it. The flatbed trucks were loaded with tiny logs and this particular section of track took the freight train round the edge of the table to a miniature logging mill, where miniature circular saws cut the miniature logs into miniature planks of wood. Measle liked the little green freight train the best because it looked the friendliest of all the trains. It didn't seem quite so menacing as most of the others did—particularly the biggest one of all, which was a grimy, oily monster locomotive, with a dented cowcatcher on the front and three dusty Pullman coaches behind it.

So, the little green freight train it would be.

Measle put his hand on the third knob from the left and gently turned it. On the other side of the table, the little green freight train started to move slowly down its section of track. Measle turned the knob a little more and the freight train picked up speed. It was moving away from him, towards the far end of the table. In a few seconds, it would make the long turn at the end of the table and chug towards him and Measle intended stopping it at its usual station—the logging mill, a few feet away from where he sat. He watched as it began to take the bend and he turned the knob a little more and the wheels of the freight train began to spin faster.

Measle was concentrating so hard on what he was doing that he didn't see something which would have scared him badly. What he didn't see was this: the monster locomotive, with its dented cowcatcher and its three Pullman coaches, had begun to move out of its siding and onto the main track. It did so quite silently and, at first, quite slowly—and, since Measle had his back turned away from it, he didn't see or hear anything.

The little freight train was now clattering towards him, down the long straight section of track on the very edge of the table. Measle decided to let it keep its speed up and stop it by the logging mill at the very last minute, which was something he'd seen Basil do lots of times. He watched carefully as the freight train clicked and chuffed its way towards him. The track here was quite long and there was plenty of time to get ready for the stop—but then, out of the corner of his eye, Measle saw the monster locomotive.

It had joined the main track—the same one the freight train was on—and was now racing towards the smaller engine, its pistons flying, its smokestack belching and its oily wheels turning so fast that they seemed to blur. Measle gasped in horror. How could that have happened? He hadn't touched the knob that controlled that section of the track—he'd never intended to, because he'd never liked the look of the monster locomotive and hadn't planned on using it at all. *Quickly— which one was the locomotive's controller? It was the fifth, wasn't it? Or was it the fourth?* Measle reached for the fifth knob and turned it hard—but

nothing happened. If anything, both trains seemed to speed up. Measle twisted the fourth knob and the two trains seemed to lean forward towards each other as they accelerated. He reached for both knobs and twisted them this way and that—and, when nothing happened, he twisted again and harder this time—and both knobs came away in his hands. Frantically, he tried to push them back on to their spindles but, for some reason, they wouldn't fit so Measle grabbed the spindles themselves and tried to turn *them* but his fingers slipped on the oily metal and he couldn't get a proper grip. In desperation, he reached for the Power On knob and tried to twist it—but the knob refused to budge. Measle grasped it with both hands and strained with all his strength.

It wouldn't move.

And all the time he was trying to turn this knob or that, the two trains were accelerating towards each other. A head-on collision was inevitable. And Measle was powerless to stop it.

'WHAT ISSS GOING ON?'

The voice came from behind him and Measle whipped round on the tall stool, almost falling off it in his fright. There, in the doorway, stood Basil Tramplebone. His fish eyes were staring and his long, bony fingers were clenched into fists and, for a moment, Measle thought he saw a trace of red on Basil's chalky cheeks.

'WHAT HAVE YOU BEEN DOING?'

Measle tried to say something—anything—but his voice wouldn't work. His tongue felt swollen and his teeth felt numb and he didn't seem able to breathe. Behind him, he could hear the clatter as the two trains raced towards each other—but he couldn't turn and watch because Basil's fish eyes were staring at him and Basil's bony fingers were curled into fists and, yes—two spots of angry red were standing out on Basil's white cheeks.

Suddenly, Basil's gaze switched from Measle's face to the train set. Measle saw Basil's eyes widen and the two angry spots of red disappear—and then Basil's whole face went a strange shade of grey, like a corpse.

And then Basil did a very odd thing. He opened his mouth and said something. To Measle, it sounded a bit like 'Sssplzzxcffft Gjriuvriok Ssskargranglio!'—a kind of snaky hiss, mixed with a kind of throat clearing, mixed with a kind of teeth grinding, mixed with a kind of nose blowing sort of sound, which was as disgusting a noise as Measle had ever heard—and, at the same moment that Basil was making this bloodcurdling noise, a strange glint of green flame appeared in his eyes and, a second later, two very bright green beams of light, like twin lasers, suddenly shot out from his pupils. The beams missed Measle by a centimetre, zipping past his face with a sizzling sound and making the air near his nose smell of burned rubber—and Measle cowered on the high stool and squeezed his eyes shut and put his hands over his ears, because Basil had never done anything like this before and Measle was suddenly very frightened indeed.

With his eyes tightly closed and his ears covered, Measle didn't hear the crash of the two trains. He didn't hear or see anything for several seconds and he began to wonder why nothing was happening. Even with his ears covered, it seemed to be awfully quiet. *Surely Basil was going to hit him? And, if so, why hadn't he done so already? What was going on?* The seconds ticked by and at last Measle's curiosity got the better of him and he cautiously opened his eyes.

And then, he wished he hadn't.

Basil was standing very close to him and smiling. Measle had never seen Basil smiling before. He hoped he never would again. Basil's smile was ghastly. Usually, when people smile, the skin at the corner of their eyes wrinkles at the same time, which makes them look friendly. Basil's eyes didn't wrinkle at all. They stayed exactly the same as always—big and round and fishy—and very, very cold. His thin, pale lips were stretched wide, revealing a row of long, yellow teeth. The teeth at the sides of his mouth were even longer and they came to a sharp point and, for a moment, Measle thought that Basil might be a vampire. But surely vampires only had one set of pointed teeth —one on each side? Basil had *three* pointed teeth on each side, which made him look a bit like an alligator—

'Ssso—we like playing with Basil's trains, do we?'

Measle swallowed hard. He'd never been so frightened in his life. 'I'm s-sorry, Mr Tramplebone, s-sir,' he managed to stammer.

'Sssorry?'

'I didn't mean for them to crash, r-really I didn't.'

'Crash? There has been no crash, boy. Look for yoursssself.'

Measle did as he was told. He swivelled round on the tall stool and stared at the train set. It was true. There was no sign of a crash. In fact, the section of track where the two trains *should* have been (lying, as Measle imagined they would be, in a tangled pile of wreckage) was empty. Measle looked around the train set in wonder and he saw that the monster locomotive was back in its siding and the little green freight train was back at its starting point, right over there on the far side of the huge table. The humming sound of the electricity was gone and all was quiet and peaceful and in its right and proper place.

'Mind you,' said Basil, his voice a whisper, very close to Measle's ear, 'mind you, there *would* have been a crash. A very nasssty crash, had I not arrived in the nick of time. And do you know how I arrived here in the nick of time, Measle?'

'N-no, sir.'

'Then I shall tell you. I arrived in the nick of time because, halfway to the bank, I realized that today is *Sssunday*. Sssunday, Measle. And you know what Sssunday means, don't you, Measle?'

'N-no, sir.'

'Sssunday means that the banksss are *closed*, Measle. Including *our* bank, Measle. Ssso—it follows that we never had a call from the man at the bank thisss morning, doesn't it, Measle?'

'Y-yes, s-sir.'

'It follows that you made the ssstory up, doesn't it, Measle?'

'Y-yes, s-sir.'

'You lied to me, didn't you, Measle? You told me a falsssehood. And you tampered with the telephone, didn't you, Measle?'

'I'm really, r-really sorry, Mr Tramplebone, sir.'

Basil patted Measle gently on his shoulder and Measle could feel the cold of Basil's fingers through the thin material of his shirt. 'Of courssse you're sssorry,' whispered Basil. 'And quite sssoon, you're going to be even sssorrier.'

A bone-chilling coldness flooded through Measle's body—and, at the same time, he could feel beads of sweat oozing out on his face. He took a deep, shuddering breath. 'What are you g-going to do?'

'Ah—there's the quessstion. What am I going to do? Well, Measle—I have always believed that the punishment should fit the crime. Do you believe that, Measle?'

'I s-suppose so, sir.'

'You sssuppose so? Good. I sssuppose ssso too. Very well—the punishment for playing with my train ssset—without my permission—is that you will play *in* my train ssset, with my *full* permission, for the ressst of your life.'

What could he mean?

'P-play with your train set, sir?' stammered Measle.

'No, boy. You mussst try and lissten when people talk to you. Not play *with* my train ssset. Play *in* my train ssset. For ever and ever and ever. Now, sssit perfectly ssstill and you won't get hurt.'

And then Basil leaned very close to Measle—and he breathed softly into Measle's face.

Measle tried hard not to, but he screwed up his face as though he'd just eaten a lemon. Basil's breath was foul. It smelt of dead fish and old mattresses and the insides of ancient sneakers—and Measle tried to lean away from the stench but Basil kept on breathing at him, until it seemed impossible to Measle that such a thin chest could contain so much air—and when Measle felt sure that Basil couldn't possibly breathe out any more without taking a breath *in*, Basil simply went on producing this soft, disgusting smelling breeze and blowing it gently into Measle's face. Measle tried to hold his breath, so he wouldn't have to smell it, but eventually he was forced to take a great gulp of air and, if anything, the smell was worse.

And Basil seemed to be getting bigger. The more he breathed out, the bigger Basil seemed to grow. Now he was towering over Measle, his head the size of a bus—*but that was impossible, surely? A bus would never fit in the attic*—and for a moment, Measle dragged his eyes away from Basil's staring, goldfish eyes and looked about him.

Basil wasn't getting bigger. Measle was getting smaller.

Already, the stool on which he'd been sitting stretched away on either side of him, as if it wasn't a stool at all, but more like a broad table. And now his feet no longer dangled a few centimetres from the floor. Now, the floor was a long, long way down and Measle appeared to be sitting on the edge of a high cliff, looking down at a drop that, if he fell, would certainly kill him.

Measle shuddered and scrambled back from the edge of the stool—and still Basil went on breathing over him; and now the breeze was becoming a wind—and now a hurricane, which forced Measle to fall back, so that now he was lying face upward on the flat wooden surface of the stool. He glanced to one side, trying to turn his face away from the dreadful smell, and he saw that the edge of the stool seemed to be a long, long way away—

And then the hurricane stopped. Measle turned his head and stared up at Basil in horror. Basil was vast, tall as a mountain—a mountain of black, topped by the stark whiteness of his face, so that he looked to Measle like the snow-capped peak of Mount Everest.

'There, now,' said Basil, his voice a distant boom. 'We've cut you down to sssize, haven't we, Measle? Oh yesss. I should have done thiss years ago but we had to keep up appearances, didn't we? Oh yesss. But now—well, we don't really need you any more, do we? You see, two weeks ago, our bank appointed a new bank manager. Oh yesss. And our new bank manager, Mr Griswold Gristle, is one of us—well, one of *me*, I should say—and a very, very friendly fellow indeed—at least to *me*. We had a deliciousss conversssation at the beginning of lassst week, Mr Gristle and I. And well, the upshot of it all was, that you were far too young to even *have* any money. So all your lovely money is now in my control, Measle. It's mine, mine, *mine*. Ssso you sssee, dear boy—you are now sssuperfluousss to requirementsss.'

Measle felt like crying but he didn't. Measle had finished with crying. He'd done a lot of it when he was younger but it hadn't changed a thing, so one day he'd simply stopped crying and hadn't cried since. Instead, he lay quite still, waiting to see what Basil would do next.

Basil said, 'Ssstay there, Measle. Don't move a muscle. Don't even blink, dear boy.'

Measle thought that was an unnecessary thing to say. Where could he go? He was lying on a flat, wooden plain, surrounded on all sides by a long, distant drop to the floor far beneath him. He watched as Basil moved away, to the other side of the attic. A moment later, he was back, looming huge over Measle. In his enormous right hand—it was the size of a house—he was holding something bright and silvery. The hand came slowly down towards Measle and Measle saw that the bright, silvery object was a pair of tweezers— the same tweezers that Basil used when he was performing some particularly delicate task on his train set, like putting a new tree in place or rearranging the chips of coal in the coal yard. Now —to Measle—the tweezers looked gigantic; each arm of the instrument was as long as an oar and the points were coming steadily towards him— 'Lie quite ssstill, Measle,' boomed Basil. 'Thisss won't hurt if you lie quite ssstill.'

Measle did as he was told. He'd learned never to argue with Basil. Besides, Basil never lied about anything. It was the only good thing you could say about Basil. Of course, the truth from Basil was never a *pleasant* truth—but it was always the truth. Measle knew that, if Basil said anything at all, it was always nasty and always true. If Basil said that poisonous blue frogs would fall from the black cloud that hung permanently over the gloomy house, you could be pretty sure that, before the day was out, the drains and the gutters would be full of very poisonous blue frogs—so, if Basil said it wouldn't hurt, then it wouldn't.

It didn't hurt—but it was unpleasant all the same. Measle watched the ends of the tweezers touch the front of his shirt—he felt the ends of the tweezers pinch together a wad of the material—then a pulling sensation as he was gently lifted up by his collar. Up and up he went, until the top of the stool was far beneath him and the attic floor even further. Measle kept very still. He knew that if he struggled, there was a good chance that his old shirt would split and that he'd drop away—and falling from this great height would certainly kill him. So he froze like a statue, his eyes wide open, praying that the collar of his shirt would hold.

Basil swung his enormous arm and Measle saw the great table top glide far beneath him—the forest, the little wooden cabins, the railway tracks, the sad, grey train yards with their sad, grey stations—and, finally, the mound of coal chips in its own little, fenced-in yard.

Measle felt himself going down. The ground seemed to rush towards him and he closed his eyes, expecting to feel a sickening crunch as his body hit—but, at the last moment, he felt a sudden slowing down in his descent and he opened his eyes just wide enough to see that he was about to be deposited right in the middle of the coal heap.

Basil placed him carefully on the very top of the

mound and then opened the tweezers and the strain on Measle's shirt collar was released.

'You always were sssuch a dirty boy,' said Basil, his voice rumbling like a distant thunderstorm. 'Now, you're even dirtier.'

'Why are you doing this?' shouted Measle.

'What was that? A little sssqueak from a dirty little mouse? You'll have to ssspeak up, Measle—your voice is ssso tiny now, I can't hear you at all.'

Measle struggled to his feet, glaring up at the black mountain that was Basil.

'Listen—I'm sorry I played with the train set!' he yelled, as loudly as he could. 'I'll never do it again!'

'Ah—that'sss better. I can jussst about hear you now.' Basil lowered his huge head, until his white face seemed to fill the whole sky. 'Not play with my train ssset? Ever again? But, Measle, my dear boy—you're welcome! Play in it as long as you like! Play in it for ever! There's ssso much to do and ssso many things to sssee! Forests to explore, houses to live in, people to talk to! Of courssse, I'm afraid they won't talk back because they can't—they're only made of plassstic—but at leasst they won't interrupt you when you tell them your life ssstory, will they? I do ssso hate it when people interrupt, don't you?'

He's mad, thought Measle. And then, because the thought was so strong, Measle raised his head and shouted, 'You're mad!'

Basil smiled his terrible smile, revealing all six pointed, yellow teeth. 'Well, of courssse I am, Measle. And how very sssweet of you to sssay ssso. After that lovely compliment, I'm almossst tempted to let you go. But no—I think not. If I did, I wouldn't be mad, would I? And we can't have that, now can we? You sssee—being mad is such enormousss *fun*! Enjoy yoursssself, young Measle. I'm going to leave you now—but I shall be back later, to sssee how you're getting along.'

Basil turned away—and then he paused and turned back again.

'One more thing, Measle—don't worry about food and drink. You will not ssstarve. If you look carefully, you'll find sssomething to eat. Sssomething very tasssty, I promissse. Bye-bye now.'

Basil moved swiftly away towards the attic door and Measle felt a sudden wind as a great mass of air rushed to fill the space that Basil had left behind him. He heard the attic door open, then close—a deep silence filled the room and Measle felt as alone as he'd ever felt in his life. He was about to climb down the steep, crumbly side of the coal heap, when he heard the attic door open again, and Basil's hissing whisper.

'Oh, Measle—jussst one more thing. A tiny word of warning. Ssstay under cover at night. It's not sssafe during the hours of darkness—the long hours of darkness. Not for a little mouse-like creature sssuch as you. It's very dangerousss for a little insssect-thing sssuch as you. Hide at night, Measle. Hide well. Hide from the thing in the rafters, Measle.'

There was a low ssss-sss-sss sound. For a moment, Measle couldn't imagine what it might be. Then, he realized—it was Basil laughing.

The attic door closed again and the silence returned.

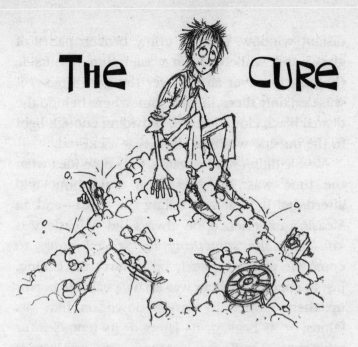

THE CURE

Measle sat very still, on the top of the coal pile, for a long time. He hardly dared to breathe—because what Basil had said confirmed his worst fears. There *was* something up there in the rafters of the attic. Something dreadful. Something that would do him harm. Something that he must avoid at all costs.

Some *thing*.

After a while, Measle's paralysed brain started to work again. Basil had said that the danger came during the long hours of darkness—which, of course, meant at night-time. Basil never lied—which meant that Measle was safe during the day. It was still daylight up here in the attic. Measle could see, at the far end of the long room, the distant window, with its grimy, broken panes of glass—and, while the sun wasn't shining outside (because it never shone over the grim house) it was certainly there, hidden somewhere behind the dismal black cloud but still providing enough light to the outside world to show that it existed.

Measle didn't have a watch, so had no idea what the time was. He guessed it was about mid afternoon. If Basil was telling the truth—and, in Measle's experience, he always did—Measle was safe from the *something* for several hours to come. He glanced quickly up towards the ceiling, just to check that there was no unspeakable horror up there, poised to swoop down on him—its talons, or its beak, or its fangs, or its tentacles (or whatever terrifying features it possessed) stretched out to grab him. It was like looking up at a stormy sky. He was so tiny now—and the ceiling was so very far away—that the distant rafters were almost lost to view in the gloom. He peered upwards, scanning the darkness. There was nothing up there—at least, nothing he could see, so, feeling far from safe but just safe enough to make a move off the coal heap, he inched himself down the side of the mound, until he arrived on the ground below.

Through his fear, Measle couldn't help being amazed at the realism of his surroundings. Apart from the coal heap, with its actual lumps of coal, the fence that surrounded it looked perfect in every detail. The wooden planks even had little knot holes in them and the whole thing was covered with a thin layer of coal dust, just as it would be if the fence was full-sized. It was a drab and dirty place and Measle decided that anywhere else on the huge table was probably going to be an improvement; so he headed for a gap in the fence and, a moment later, found himself in the heart of the railway yards.

There were two small freight train engines standing next to each other in the yard. One had no wagons behind it. The other had three empty coal trucks linked to its tender. Both were filthy—covered with the kind of black grime you would expect to see on locomotives that were stationed near a coal yard. Measle gave them no more than a glance—he knew that they would be there, having seen them there only minutes before, when he was still full-sized. Instead, he picked his way across the railway tracks, heading for the miniature town beyond them. The ground was lumpy and uneven, covered with the sort of rubbish you might expect in an old railway yard—bits of twisted metal, rotting wooden crates, rusting machine parts—and Measle had to walk carefully, in order not to trip over something.

At last he reached the edge of the railway yard. There was a building here. A long, low, brick building, with a slate roof. It looked very real and Measle stopped for a moment to admire it. The bricks looked old and several of the slates were missing from the roof. The glass in most of the windows was cracked or broken and the whole building looked shabby and neglected. Measle picked his way towards it. There was a door, hanging ajar on sagging hinges and Measle cautiously poked his head inside and looked around. The building was empty. There was no furniture, no pictures, no rubbish, no nothing— simply the plain brick walls and a bare, rather new-looking wooden floor. Measle looked more closely at the floor. It was plywood—and it looked very much like the same kind of plywood that the huge table was made of. Measle knew what the huge table was made of because, once, when he and Basil were in the attic, the vibration of a passing train had caused a pine tree to fall off the edge of the table and down onto the floor. Basil had told Measle to pick it up. Measle had bent down and picked up the tree and, for a moment, had lingered there, looking up at the underside of the table. He saw that it was supported on eight rows of wooden trestles and that the table top itself was made of many sheets of smooth, white birch plywood which rested securely on the trestles.

The floor of the shabby building—in which he now stood—looked as if it was made from the same birch plywood. In that moment, Measle learned something—Basil only cared about what you could see. If it was visible from above, everything about the train set was correct, down to the smallest detail. If it *wasn't* visible from above, Basil didn't care about it. Measle tucked this bit of information away in his brain and walked quickly through the empty building to another door on the far side of the bare room. He pushed it open and found himself—as he knew he would —in a street of small, sooty houses.

At the far end of the street—which Measle knew was quite near the edge of the great table— was a pair of plastic figures. Measle remembered them; one was the man in the blue coat and the yellow helmet, sitting on the side of the pit, holding the electrical cables. The other figure, directly behind him, was the man with the bucket of water. Measle decided to take a closer look, so he walked quickly down the street towards them. As he got nearer, he noticed that there was a considerable difference between the two plastic figures. At close range, the man with the bucket of water was quite crudely modelled. His paintwork was rough and the seam (where his two halves had been joined together in the factory) was plain to see, running down the middle of his face and on down his chest.

The man with the yellow helmet was something else entirely. He too was obviously made of plastic, but the hair and the clothes—and even the lines of ageing on the face of the man, and the greying hair poking out from under the yellow helmet—looked amazingly realistic. There was no seam running down his body either—so Measle wondered if perhaps Basil hadn't bought him from one of his model railway catalogues at all, but had actually made him himself? If so—well, it was a brilliant piece of craftsmanship. There was even a battered steel toolbox by the man's side—something Measle had never noticed before.

A little further on from where Measle was standing was the edge of the table and, near the edge, there was a small scattering of yellow objects and a broad puddle of pink liquid. For a moment, Measle couldn't imagine what they could be— then he realized what they were: glazed doughnut crumbs and spilled pink lemonade, left there by Basil after one of his binges.

Measle suddenly felt hungry. His meagre lunch seemed a long time ago and it hadn't been much to speak of anyway. He'd always longed for a taste of Basil's glazed doughnuts—and a sip of Basil's pink lemonade—and now, at last, he could eat and drink his fill of them. Perhaps, he thought, there was something to be said for being two centimetres tall—back when he was full-sized, what lay before him would have been nothing but a few crumbs and a single drop but now—in this miniature state—it was a feast that could last him several days. Obviously, that was what Basil had meant when he'd said that Measle would find plenty to eat and drink and all he had to do was find it.

Well, he'd found it. Measle moved past the still, silent figures of the two men and, when he reached the scattered doughnut crumbs, he bent down and picked up the nearest, brought it up to his nose and sniffed. Yes, it was certainly doughnut. He opened his mouth—

'Nurrr.'

The sound, very quiet and muffled, had come from behind him. Measle turned quickly. Apart from the two plastic men, the street was empty. Measle shook his head. He must have imagined it. He opened his mouth again—

'Nurrr!'

This time, Measle knew he hadn't imagined it. The sound came from close by—right where the figures of the men were placed. Was it possible that one of them was trying to say something to him? To test this theory, Measle stared hard at the figures and slowly raised the doughnut crumb to his mouth.

'Nurrr! Nurrr! Nurrr!'

It was the man with the yellow helmet. His mouth had moved—at least, one small corner of it. It had opened just wide enough for the sound to come out. There was no question about it—the voice had come from the plastic man and he was trying to say something. Measle took a couple of careful steps towards the figure and then stopped. There was something creepy about all this and Measle—for the second time that day—felt very scared.

'Wh-what did you say?' he stammered.

The corner of the mouth opened again. 'Own eat.'

'What?'

'Own eat 'onut. Own 'ink 'enonade.'

Measle frowned. It sounded as if the man was trying to say 'Don't eat doughnut—don't drink lemonade.'

'You don't want me to eat this?' said Measle, holding up the doughnut crumb.

'Ri'. Own eat. Own 'ink. Nedder, nedder nedder.'

'Why not?'

'End uck like 'ee.'

That one took a bit of thinking about. A moment later, Measle got it. 'End up like you?'

'Ri'.'

Measle stared at the model. It was very strange being told not to do something by a plastic man. In fact, it was so strange that Measle forgot his fear and took two steps closer. He peered up at the man's face. There was no question about it—while amazingly realistic, he was still made entirely of plastic (or, at least, something that looked exactly *like* plastic) except, perhaps, for that small corner of his mouth. The rest of his face was smooth and shiny. The eyes stared blankly off into the distance —but the corner of the mouth looked a little different. There seemed to be something human about it, something alive—

'How can you talk? You're a plastic model, aren't you?'

' 'Ostly. Just a lil 'it left now.'

'You mean—you're *alive*?'

'Not for 'uch longer. Soon I'll 'ee all 'lastic.'

'Soon you'll be all plastic?'

'Yesh.'

'But—how? Why?'

'The 'onuts. The 'enonade. '*Oison*.'

'The doughnuts and the lemonade are poison?'

'Ri'. They turn 'oo into 'lastic.'

Measle looked about him. 'But there's nothing else to eat. I'll starve to death.'

' 'Etter than 'eing 'lastic.'

Measle felt all hope draining from his mind. He knew he could probably last a few days but, eventually, he would become so weak for want of food and water that he'd no longer be able to walk, let alone search for food that wasn't there. He sank slowly to his knees and, as he did so, he felt a pressure against his thigh from something in his pocket. He reached in and his fingers touched paper—of course!—it was the bag of carrots he'd taken from the refrigerator earlier that same day.

Measle pulled the bag out of his pocket and looked inside. He counted the carrots—twelve old, wrinkled things, some still crusted with the soil they'd grown in. If he was careful, he could make them last maybe six days—but after that?

He reached in and took out the cleanest.

' 'Ossat 'oo got 'ere?'

'Just an old carrot.'

'A 'arrot?' There was a combination of amazement and longing in the man's voice as if, at first, he couldn't believe what he'd heard and, then, if he *had* heard it right, he couldn't believe that something so wonderful could be so close to him.

Measle looked up at him and said, 'You want some?'

There was a pause, then the man, in a tone of great sadness, said,' 'On't 'ink I can chew it. 'Outh don't 'erk.'

'Your mouth doesn't work?'

'Ri'.'

'I could cut it up for you—that is, if you can still swallow?'

There was another pause and then Measle heard a gulping sound.

'I can do 'at,' said the man, sounding suddenly much happier.

'Good,' said Measle. Then he said, 'Um—trouble is, I haven't got a knife.'

' 'Ook in de 'ool'ox.'

Look in the toolbox. Measle squatted down and

opened the battered toolbox. Inside, there was a lift-out tray with lots of small compartments. The compartments held electrical connectors and screws and staples and nails—but nothing to cut a carrot with.

'Unnerneath,' said the plastic man.

Measle lifted out the tray. Down in the bottom of the box was a jumbled pile of tools—hammers and saws and screwdrivers and drills and chisels — and, right at the very bottom, was a folding penknife. It had a handle made from deer horn, and a long, curved blade. It was the sort of knife Measle had always wanted—but Basil would never have let him have a penknife. Basil wouldn't let him have anything of his own, apart from his few dirty old clothes. Measle stared at the knife for a moment, a grin spreading over his face.

' 'Oo want 'at?' said the man.

Measle felt himself going red. He nodded.

'Iss yours.'

Measle went even redder. He'd never had a present before. Measle didn't know when his birthday was and, even if he *had* known, he was sure that Basil would've ignored it. And as for Christmas—

'Thank you very much.'

' 'Oo're 'elcome.'

Measle wiped a patch of roadway in front of him with the end of his sleeve, until it was as clean as he could get it. Then he put the carrot down on the spot, opened the penknife and began to chop the carrot into small pieces.

'When was the last time you had something to eat?' he asked.

' 'On't know—'aybe six years. 'Onuts and 'enonade.'

'Six *years*? You must be starving!'

' 'En oo're 'lastic, 'oo don't 'tarve. Jus' get 'ery, 'ery 'ungry.'

'Well, here you are.'

Measle scooped up the chopped carrot and carefully, piece by piece, pushed the little cubes into the corner of the man's mouth.

'Good. 'Ery good,' said the man, between swallows. ' 'Etter 'an 'onuts and 'enonade.'

Measle went on feeding the man until all the chopped carrot was gone.

' 'Ank 'oo,' said the man.

Then Measle saw a very odd thing. The man began to move the side of his mouth in and out, in and out—and then, suddenly, he was moving his whole mouth and now the rest of it no longer looked as if it was made of hard plastic—now it was a truly human mouth and the man opened it and said, quite clearly and without any of the muffled sound, 'Thank you very much, Measle.'

And then the man's eyebrows shot up to the top of his forehead, as if he was as surprised at this new sound as Measle was—who was very surprised indeed.

Measle said, 'You can talk properly now!'

'Looks like I can,' said the man and he opened his mouth wide, stretching his jaw muscles and wiggling his tongue. 'Well, who'd have thought it? Must be the effects of the carrot.'

'The *carrot* did it?'

'Can't think what else,' said the man, suddenly dropping the electric cables, raising his right arm and touching his face with his hand.

'You can move!' shouted Measle.

'So I can!'

The man stared at his hand. He flexed the fingers, watching them bend and straighten. Then he lifted his left arm and scratched his ear. 'I've been dying to do that for six years,' he said. 'Now, let's see about the legs, shall we?'

Slowly, the man pulled himself to his feet. Then he leaned forward and lifted one foot and took a step forward. He swayed and grabbed Measle's shoulder. 'A bit wobbly, but I think I'm getting better.'

Measle stared at him in wonder. There, standing by his side and leaning heavily on his shoulder, was a living, breathing human man, with all trace of plastic gone from his appearance.

'I can't believe a carrot could do that,' he said. 'It doesn't make any sense.'

The man looked down at him and smiled. 'It makes the same kind of sense as doughnuts and lemonade turning you into plastic, don't you think? It makes as much sense as this whole situation. I mean, look at us! We're two centimetres tall, prisoners on top of a table, stuck in a model railway set. If that makes any sense to you, Measle, then you must be pretty peculiar.'

'I suppose I am—a bit,' said Measle.

'No, you're not,' said the man, patting Measle on the shoulder. 'You're a hero, that's what you are. Look, you brought me back to life, didn't you? That makes you a hero, Measle.'

'How do you know my name?'

The man looked gloomy. 'Well, that's part of the cruelty of it all. We may be plastic, but that doesn't mean we can't still hear and see. I've watched you, watching us, all the time I've been here. Couldn't move, could hardly speak, and hungry as a horse— but I could see and hear everything that goes on. That's how I know your name—listening to Basil Tramplebone. "Pick that up, Measle." "Put that down, Measle." "Sit still, Measle." And, I'll tell you something else, young Measle—I don't think that Basil is quite human.'

'I'm absolutely sure he's not,' said Measle.

'Then what do you think he is?'

'I don't know,' said Measle. 'And I don't think I want to know.'

The man nodded thoughtfully. Then he took a

deep breath and said, 'Come on. Let's head for the centre of town. There may be a few others we can work the carrot magic on. Know the way, do you?'

Measle nodded. The two of them set off, walking quickly back along the street towards a crossroads in the distance. Measle remembered that, by turning right there, the side street would lead them to the main part of the town. As they walked, he asked the man his name.

'Frank,' said the man. 'Frank Hunter.'

'How did you get here?'

'Same way you did. It seems to happen to anybody who makes Mr Tramplebone angry. See— I'm an electrician. I put in the wiring for the train set. It was all built and ready to go, except for the electrics. When I'd finished, he seemed happy with what I'd done. Then I gave him the bill. All of a sudden, he wasn't happy at all. In fact, he refused to pay it. We got into an argument. Next thing I know, I'm two centimetres tall, wandering about in his train set. I ate the crumbs of doughnuts and drank the drops of lemonade—all the time trying to keep out of his sight—and slowly, I got stiffer and stiffer and stiffer, until I couldn't move at all. Of course, there's something special about Basil's doughnuts and his lemonade. I mean to say, we all know that stuff's bad for you—but not *that* bad.'

'But what about how I found you? I mean, you with the electric wires—and the man with the bucket of water? What was all that about?'

Frank shook his head. 'I dunno,' he said. 'Basil likes to change things around and, once you're unable to move, then he can put you into any position he likes. A few weeks ago, I was up a telegraph pole. Before that, he had me changing a light bulb in one of the street lamps. Then Basil started rearranging stuff again, and there I am being menaced by a man with a bucket of water. Of course, I was in no danger but all the same—it was a bit creepy, knowing he was behind me like that.'

Measle stopped so suddenly that Frank walked on a couple of steps before he realized that Measle was no longer by his side. He too stopped and turned, looking back at Measle.

'What is it?'

'I know which ones to rescue,' said Measle.

'You do? Who?'

'They're the ones Basil put into weird situations. There's a bunch of them and they're all in some sort of danger. Well, *pretend* danger. Just like you. There's one in the town square, there's a couple in the forest—one near the second station—'

Frank grinned. 'Well, come on then,' he said. 'What are we waiting for? Town square first, I think. It's nearest, isn't it?'

They walked quickly to the town square. There was the suggestion of a park here, with a worn patch of grass (in reality, it was painted sandpaper) and a few sad looking trees, made from papier-mâché. In the middle of the square was a statue, set high on a stone base.

The statue was of a man and a woman. The woman was kneeling by the man's side and her arm was thrown across her face, as if she couldn't bear to see what was in front of her. The man stood straight and tall beside her, his right hand extended forward, his palm facing outward, as if he was trying to stop something that was approaching. At the bottom of the statue, carved into the stone base, were some words. Measle had often tried to read the words when he was watching Basil play with his trains, but the writing was too small and too far away from where he used to sit, so he'd never known what they said. Now, two centimetres tall and standing in the shadow of the statue, he could read them quite clearly.

IN MEMORIAM

VENI, VIDI, VICI

REQUIESCAT IN PACE

HA HA HA

'What does it mean?' asked Measle, looking up at the statue.

'Well,' said Frank, slowly, 'I think it's Latin. I know the first one. It means "In Memory". I don't know what the one underneath it means. The next means "Rest In Peace".'

'And the "HA HA HA"?'

Frank looked suddenly angry. 'I think that's Basil laughing,' he said, quietly. 'Come on—let's rescue that woman from the plastic tiger, shall we?'

They approached the steps of the Town Hall, where the figures of the crouching woman and the menacing Bengal tiger were positioned. As they passed the tiger, Measle could clearly see that it was just a shop-bought model—the most obvious evidence being the rough paintwork on its body and face and the raised seam that ran down the length of its back. The woman looked much more realistic. She was dressed in a smart suit—a grey skirt, with a matching grey jacket, and a white blouse. Her shoes were black, with high heels, and there was an expensive-looking leather handbag beside her. She was leaning forward, her elbows on the ground, her head buried in her hands. Frank knelt down in front of her.

'Miss? Can you talk, miss?'

'Yes,' said the woman, her voice very soft and low, but quite distinct. 'But I'm not a "miss". I'm a lady.'

'Of course you are, miss,' said Frank, kindly.

'No, you don't understand,' muttered the woman. 'My name is Lady Grant, you see. Lady Mary Grant.'

'Oh,' said Frank. He turned his head and winked at Measle. 'So sorry, Lady Grant.'

'Oh, please help me!' said Lady Grant. 'I've been

staring at the ground for such a long time ... and I can't move at all ... oh, please ... whoever you are ... can you do something?'

Frank grinned at Measle. 'Let me have a carrot, Measle,' he said. 'No, on second thoughts, just a little bit of a carrot. It may be enough—she's not as bad as I was—and we've got to make them last.'

Measle took the smallest carrot out of the paper bag, opened the penknife and cut a small chip off it. He handed it to Frank and Frank gently pushed the chip into the woman's mouth.

'Can you bite that?' he asked.

'Yes, I think so. What is it? And I do hope you washed your hands? Oh—it's a carrot. Why are you giving me a carrot?'

'You'll see,' said Frank.

There was a crunching sound, as the woman began to chew. She said, 'It's all gritty. And I don't really terribly care for raw carrots—' And then she stopped talking because, slowly, her head was beginning to raise itself and, a moment later, she was sitting upright.

'Oh, how marvellous,' she said, in a grand voice, smiling in astonishment. 'This is wonderful. I can't thank you enough.' She looked closely at Frank and her eyes widened. 'I know you,' she said. 'You're the man near the coal yard, aren't you? When I could still move, I saw you there.'

Frank said, 'The name's Hunter, Lady Grant. Frank Hunter.' He touched Measle on the shoulder and gently pushed him forward. 'And this is your rescuer.'

She stared at Measle, her eyes widening with growing horror. 'Oh, my goodness. You're the boy, aren't you? The giant boy! You're in league with that revolting Tramplebone creature!'

'Not in league at all, Lady Grant,' said Frank. 'And not a giant any more, as you may have noticed. Basil's done to him what he's done to all of us. He just rescued you. This is Measle.'

'Yes, *Measle*,' cried Lady Grant. 'That's your unfortunate name, isn't it? So you're not Tramplebone's friend then?'

Measle shook his head. 'I hate him,' he muttered.

Lady Grant clasped her hands under her chin. 'Oh, I'm so glad. I mean, I know one isn't supposed to hate anybody—but I'm afraid I've had to make an exception in Tramplebone's case. Well, Measle—what an odd name—I don't know how to thank you.'

Measle's face went pink. Nobody had ever said 'thank you' to him in his entire life and, now, he'd been thanked twice in the last few minutes and he really wasn't used to it. He opened his mouth to say something but Lady Grant raised her hand. 'No, no,' she said. 'No need to say anything. Now, I wonder what I could do to repay you—once we're out of this revolting situation, I mean.' She gazed at him, her eyes slowly taking him in. She sniffed and then wrinkled her nose. 'Well, perhaps a visit to a bathroom to start with—and then, my dear, well, something will simply *have* to be done about it!'

'Done about what?' said Measle.

'Dear boy—your hair! I've never seen anything quite like it in my entire life. It looks as though somebody's been chopping at it with a kitchen knife!'

'How did you know?' said Measle.

Lady Grant blinked several times. 'You mean—I was *right*? Good heavens! Well, never mind—my personal hairdresser will know what to do with it.'

'So—what happened to you, Lady Grant?' asked Frank.

'Well, I'm a Borough Councillor, you see. At least, I *was* a Borough Councillor. From the Town Hall. We had sent several letters to Mr Tramplebone about the state of his house, but he never replied to any of them. I really don't care to be ignored, so I came in person—and at some inconvenience—to tell Mr Tramplebone that his house was in a terrible state of repair and that he was to do something about it. His drains, too. They were blocking the main sewer up with some sort of *revolting* green globs—'

Measle nodded. 'That's our bath water,' he said.

Lady Grant stared at Measle for a moment, as if she couldn't quite believe that he'd said that. Then she blinked and started to speak again. 'Anyway, I told him that he had to make certain repairs within the next six months, or steps would be taken against him. He just looked at me with those frightful eyes and then he started breathing on me —and his breath was *revolting*—and the next thing I know, I'm two centimetres tall, wandering about in this ridiculous little fake town.'

'See what I mean?' said Frank to Measle. 'Anybody who makes Basil angry gets it and gets it good.'

'He's a *revolting* creature, that's all I know,' said Lady Grant.

Measle Frank Lady Grant Kip

Prudence Kitty William

THE VICTIMS

During the next hour and a half, Measle, Frank, and
Lady Grant brought the remaining four people
back to life.

The first was nearby, in a long street that led
towards the forest. Measle led them to the spot
where he'd seen the tableau of the little round bald
man being chased by the angry mob. Ignoring the
plastic pursuers and their placards, they went
directly to the little man and fed him some chips of
carrot and, moments later, he dropped his heavy
suitcase and sat down heavily in the middle of the
road. He shook his head and wiped his shiny
forehead with the sleeve of his coat.

'Phew,' he gasped. 'You only just got here in time. They nearly had me.'

Measle said, 'No, they couldn't have. Honestly. They're only plastic, you see.'

The little man looked up at him and grinned. He put his right forefinger alongside his nose and tapped it knowingly. 'I know that, kid. That was a little joke, you see. I make lots of little jokes. You'll get used to it.'

He pulled himself to his feet, breathing heavily. 'Grateful thanks all round. The name's Durham. William O. Durham. Don't ask what the O stands for—'cause it doesn't stand for anything, see? "O" —geddit? Zero, in other words. Well, you've got to laugh, haven't you?'

'I don't see why,' sniffed Lady Grant.

William turned out to be a travelling salesman, who had tried to sell a set of expensive encyclopedias to Basil a year and a half ago. He'd stood on the doorstep and done his salesman chat and, when Basil had tried to close the door, William had stuck his foot in the gap. A moment later, Basil's bony hand had reached out and dragged William into the house by his shirt front and—

'What a nasty piece of work,' William said. 'Even nastier than my boss—and that's saying something. At least my boss doesn't have bad breath. Dear, oh, dear. We all got a good whiff of Basil's though, didn't we? Phew, what a stink, eh? Now then—where are my samples?'

He pulled his suitcase onto his knees and snapped open the catches. He lifted the lid and nodded with satisfaction. The case was packed tight with encyclopedias.

'All here still. Well, there's a turn up for the books.' When nobody laughed, he said, '*Books*. Turn up for the *books*. 'Cause I sell them, see? Another little joke. I've got millions of them.'

Lady Grant made a face. 'Well, perhaps we don't need to hear them all at once, Mr Durham.'

Frank broke the awkward silence that followed.

'Come on then, Measle,' he said, cheerfully. 'Let's go get the rest of them.'

Next to be rescued was the little girl. Frank pushed the three black plastic bears away from the base of the pine tree, in order to give themselves room to move. It was decided that the best thing to do was for Measle to climb up to the girl with a few carrot chips and feed them to her while she was still up in the tree. Frank gave Measle his harness—which Frank used when mending power lines at the top of telegraph poles—and showed him how to fasten it round the girl so that she wouldn't fall.

'And you be careful up there, Measle,' he said. 'We don't want to lose you.'

The pine tree was easy to climb, with lots of branches all the way up. Measle quickly reached the girl. Her arms were wrapped tightly around the trunk and her cheek was pressed hard against the rough bark. Her eyes were tight shut and when Measle touched her on the shoulder, she gasped.

'It's all right,' he whispered. 'I'm just going to tie this round you. It'll stop you falling, you see. There—now swallow this. Don't worry, you'll be all right.'

Measle fed her a small piece of carrot and a few moments later she let go of the trunk, threw her arms around his neck, and burst into tears.

'Ooh—thank you, thank you, thank you!' she sobbed.

Measle went even pinker than when Lady Grant had thanked him. The little girl's tears were soaking into his old shirt.

'Can you climb down?' he asked, hoping that this was something that Brownies could do at least as well as they could cry. The little girl sniffed and nodded, so Measle carefully untied Frank's harness and the girl scrambled down the tree in a way that suggested that tree-climbing was obviously a Brownie speciality.

Everybody clustered around her and soon she stopped crying and was able to tell her story. Her name was Kitty Webb and she had come to the house—much against her better judgement—to try and sell some Brownie biscuits to Basil. When Basil had opened the door, Kitty had taken one look at him and had then—sensibly—tried to run away. But Basil had caught her with one of his bony, yellow hands and the rest was history.

Lady Grant took a tissue from her handbag and wiped away the traces of Kitty's tears. 'What a charming uniform,' she cooed. 'So smart—quite like my designer suit. And so many badges. What a clever girl you must be.'

'Who's next, Measle?' asked Frank.

'Um—well, there's the man in the forest. Near the lake.'

'We're right behind you.'

Measle led them to the clearing. The walk took several minutes and halfway there, Lady Grant, trailing in the rear, moaned and said, 'Is it very much further? Only these shoes are not designed for walking in the woods, you see.'

William O. Durham looked back at her and laughed shortly. 'Ho! You should try carrying a suitcase of encyclopedias round, lady. Weigh half a ton, these do. Very heavy stuff, is knowledge. That's why clever people have such big heads, you see. It's all that extra weight they're lugging about.'

Soon they reached the clearing. They stood in a circle, staring at the enormous black man sitting on the tree stump. The man was huge, almost three centimetres tall (which made him, Measle calculated, over two metres in real life). His plastic chest bulged with plastic muscles, his plastic arms were as thick as trees. At first, Measle thought that the man was too far gone; there didn't seem to be any part of him that wasn't hard, unyielding plastic. When they spoke to him, there was no response.

William said, 'Do you think he's alive?'

'There's one way to find out,' said Frank. He reached into his toolbox and brought out a little round mirror on the end of a metal stick. 'I use it to see round difficult corners,' he explained. Frank put the mirror close to the plastic man's nose. Then he took it away and examined it closely. 'Look at this,' he said.

They all clustered around the little mirror. It was clouded, as if someone had breathed on it. 'His lungs are working,' said Frank. 'Question is, how do we get the carrot inside him?'

William said, 'Wait a minute. Let me have a look at my books.' He sat down on a nearby stump and opened his suitcase. He pulled out an encyclopedia, flipping quickly through the pages —then he rose and returned to the group.

'There!' he said, pointing down at a page.

It was a section on human anatomy and the picture that William was pointing at was an illustration of the inside of a man's head. It showed the brain and the nose and the mouth and the throat—and how they were all interconnected.

'Look,' said William, tracing his finger over the picture. 'See how the nose passages join up to the back of the throat? This chap is still breathing. I reckon if we can cut the carrot very small—and if the chap can sniff really hard—we might be able to get enough into him.'

'It's going to be frightfully uncomfortable for him,' said Lady Grant.

'But better than ending up solid plastic,' said Frank. 'I know—Measle got to me just in time. Another few months . . .' His voice trailed away.

William closed his encyclopedia with a bang. 'First, we're going to have to see if the chap can sniff that hard.' He moved close to the plastic figure and shouted into its face. 'Hey, old chap! Can you sniff—really *hard*?'

They all heard it—the sound of a strong intake of breath through the plastic nostrils.

'Good!' said William. He turned to Measle. 'I think we're going to need a lot of carrot for this chap—and chopped very small. As small as you can get it.'

Measle set to work. Quite soon, he had a small heap of finely chopped carrot on the ground in

front of him.
William took one
tiny piece and put it on the
palm of his hand. Then he lifted his hand close to
the man's nose. 'Right, mate,' he said. 'This might be
a bit uncomfortable—and you've got to try and
stop it going into your lungs—but it's worked for
the rest of us, so it's going to work for you too. Go
on, now—sniff as hard as you can.'

Sniff.

The tiny piece of carrot disappeared into the
plastic man's nose. A moment later, there was a
coughing, choking sound—then silence.

'You OK?' said William. 'Sniff twice if you are.'

Sniff. Sniff.

'Did it go down all right? Down into the old tum
tum?'

Sniff. Sniff.

'I guess it did,' said William. 'Ready to try again?'

Sniff. Sniff.

It took half an hour to get twenty tiny pieces of
carrot into the man and most of them were
accompanied by the coughing, choking noises.
Measle began to feel very sorry for the man—and
then he saw a sudden twitching at the corner of
the man's mouth, and the twitching turned into a
small opening in the plastic, which suddenly
wasn't plastic any more. Now, it was five
millimetres of human flesh—

William was about to put another carrot chip

into the man's nose. 'Wait!' shouted Measle. 'Look —look at his mouth!'

After that, it was easy. It still took a long time, and the pieces of carrot went in very slowly, but there was no more coughing or choking and more and more of the man's face became human, with human skin and muscles over human bone. Quite soon he was talking, in a slurred and slushy voice.

'Boy—am I glad *that's* over. You ever take food up your nose? Let me tell you—you don't want to do it. But thanks. Thanks a million. Name's Kip. Kip Lovell.'

'You've been here a very long time,' said Frank.

Kip nodded. 'I've been here since the beginning. I'm a carpenter—I built this table for Mr Tramplebone. When I'd finished, he complained that the edges were too rough, so I was up here one day, sanding them down, when suddenly he started breathing into my face—'

'So revolting,' said Lady Grant—and Measle began to wonder if perhaps '*revolting*' was her favourite word.

'Next thing I know, I'm down to the size of a nail, stuck on this table top. Tramplebone made me help him build the model. At first, he fed me properly—little bits of meat and vegetables, a drop of water now and then. But, once the place was pretty much finished, he started leaving his doughnut crumbs and his lemonade and, well— that was the end of me. I watched you all arrive. I watched you, young Measle—and I wondered how long it would be before you joined us. Now I know.'

Kip picked up his carpenter's bag and his chainsaw and the red fuel tank and rose to his feet, towering head and shoulders over the rest of them. He turned and surveyed the three plastic lumberjacks behind him. 'That Basil—he's got some sick imagination.'

'He's got a sick *everything*,' said William, packing away his encyclopedia. 'I mean to say—having breath so horrible that it shrinks a chap like me down to the size of a drawing pin. Dear, oh, dear. There must be something seriously wrong with his stomach. Stands to reason, doesn't it?'

'I don't think reason comes into it,' said Frank. 'I think, with Basil Tramplebone, you've got to throw reason out of the window.'

William shook his shiny round head. 'I'd like to throw *him* out of the window. But there's got to be a scientific explanation for all this, hasn't there?'

Lady Grant snorted. 'Well, if there is one, I'd like to hear it.'

There was a short silence, while everybody thought about this. Then William opened his mouth—but Frank got in before he could say anything.

'Is there anybody else, Measle?' he asked.

'Um—there's the old lady.'

Frank nodded. 'I remember her. Where is she?'

Measle pointed back towards the town. 'She's in a siding at the second station—the one on the branch line.'

Kip stepped into their midst. He looked up at the distant attic window. 'We'd better hurry,' he said. 'There's not much daylight left.'

By the time they reached the old lady, the light was failing fast. Hurriedly, they pushed aside the plastic figures that were clustered round her and Kip took a sharp utility knife from his tool bag and cut the ropes that bound her to the railway tracks. Her mouth was still working normally and she was able to gasp out her thanks as they lifted her clear of the rails and laid her gently on a bench on the station platform. Measle fed her some chips of carrot—he noticed that they'd used up nearly half his supply—and a few moments later the old lady was able to sit up.

Her name was Prudence Peyser and she was much older than the rest of the adults, with a mop of untidy grey hair and lots of wrinkles on her face. She was dressed in an old, green nylon anorak and a tweed skirt. A pair of sensible looking shoes were on her feet and a pair of thick woollen stockings encased her legs. When they brought her back to life and asked her who she was, she told them her name and then she said, 'I'm a wrathmonkologist.'

'A what?' said Measle.

Prudence looked embarrassed. She said, 'A wrathmonkologist. It's a silly name, I know. And a

71

lot of people think what I do is pretty silly. I go around studying wrathmonks. Most people don't know what they are—and, even if they do, they don't believe in them.'

William said, 'I never heard of them. What are wrathmonks?'

Prudence said, 'Well, you've all heard of sorcerers, I suppose?'

Everybody nodded their heads. William said, '*Heard* of 'em, yes. But if they're not in the encyclopedias—and they're not because I've read 'em all, cover to cover—well, as far as I'm concerned, they don't exist.'

'Well,' said Prudence, 'that's because the people who write the encyclopedias don't *believe* they exist. One can't really blame them, I suppose. Not in this day and age. But perhaps you'll change your minds when you hear this. Now, *sorcerers* is the general word for all three levels of wizardry—'

'Oh, there's *three* levels, are there?' said William, in a sneery voice.

Prudence sighed. 'Yes, Mr Durham, there are—and I know none of this is in your encyclopedias but then neither are *you*—and yet *you* exist, don't you?'

William opened his mouth to say something and then thought better of it. Instead, he simply said, 'Humph,' and then stared at the ground. Measle grinned inwardly. He was beginning to like this old lady.

Prudence went on, 'Now, as you probably know from the fairy stories, wizards are supposed to be reasonably good and kind, and use their powers only to improve things. Merlin was the best example, I suppose—if he ever existed, of course. There are still quite a few of them around but most of them live very quietly nowadays. They like collecting stamps and listening to classical music and mending old clocks. In fact, if you ever come across an old gentleman—or an old lady come to that, sorcerers can be male or female—if you ever come across somebody who likes doing all three of those things, then you can be pretty sure he or she is a wizard—and there's nothing much to fear from them.

'Next, we have warlocks. Warlocks are wizards who have a dark side to them—they mostly use their powers for good but sometimes they don't. Quite a lot of warlocks become lawyers, and we know about *them*, don't we? Others go into politics. You can always tell a politician who's really a warlock—they try to stop anything new happening and they don't much care for young people. They dress in very expensive clothes, drive very expensive cars, and drink a lot of very expensive wine. You don't have to fear them—just be a bit careful when you're around one.

'Last you have the wrathmonks. Wrathmonks are another thing altogether. You should be very, very frightened when you're anywhere *near* a wrathmonk. You see, wrathmonks are warlocks who have gone mad. Wizards never go mad but warlocks do occasionally (it's got something to do with all the stress in their lives, I think) and, when they do, they become wrathmonks. Thank heavens, it's quite a rare event, because there's nothing you can do with a wrathmonk. All the dark side comes pouring out of them and they're completely out of control. Wizards and warlocks hate them and are scared of them—probably because a wrathmonk's insanity is what makes them so powerful. They don't think before they act, which makes their power very pure. And pure power is unstoppable.'

'And . . . Basil is one of them?' said Frank.

'As far as I can determine—yes,' said Prudence.

'Whatever he is,' said Lady Grant, 'he's a revolting creature.'

'I don't know about all this,' said William, doubtfully. 'Wizards and warlocks and wrathmonks. What about witches, then?'

Prudence shook her grey curls. 'Witches are something else entirely, Mr Durham. They have no magical powers at all. Witchcraft is all to do with the sacred meaning of nature and is not to be confused with sorcery in any way.'

William sniffed. 'I don't know. Dear, oh, dear. I mean, it's all a bit far-fetched, isn't it?'

Frank shifted his yellow helmet off his forehead and scratched his head. 'I think if Miss Prudence says there are such things, we ought to believe in them. After all, the proof's right here.'

'I don't know,' said William, shaking his head. 'I mean—it's not *scientific*, is it? Not like my books.'

'Your books are all very well,' said Frank. 'All very well in the *real* world. But you're not in the real world now, are you? I mean—just look around you!'

William gazed gloomily at his surroundings. 'Right. You've got a point there. I suppose it's just possible these wrathmonks do, possibly, exist.'

'Of course there are wrathmonks!' cried Kitty. Everybody turned in surprise and stared at her. She'd been so quiet all this time, staying close to Measle all the way back from the forest and not saying a word to anyone. Now she blushed a deep red and stared hard at the ground. 'I believe in them,' she said, so quietly that her words could hardly be heard.

Kip nodded. 'So do I. It's crazy not to, seeing as we're all victims of one.'

Prudence looked relieved. She said, 'I'm glad you all agree. You see . . . I've been studying Basil Tramplebone for some time. Of course, I could never get near him but I'd been watching the house for six months. It was the rain cloud that gave him away. Wrathmonks always have rain clouds hanging over them. It's part of that dark side I was telling you about. Anyway, one day I got careless and Basil caught me watching the house and, quick as a flash, here I am.'

'Is Basil a very *powerful* writh—wroth—um—webfink?' asked Measle, nervously.

'*Wrathmonk*,' said Prudence. 'They're all powerful. Thank goodness, there aren't that many of them. Basil's one of the meanest and nastiest I've ever seen.'

'Is there anything that can be done—against them, I mean?' asked Frank.

Prudence shook her head. 'Not really. It's generally believed by wrathmonkologists that a wrathmonk's spell is actually stronger than he is—which means that, if there was some way of turning the wrathmonk's spell back at him, then he wouldn't be able to resist it. But as far as I know, nobody's ever succeeded in doing that, so it's only a theory.'

There was a grim silence, while everybody thought about this. Then Prudence said, 'By the way, has anybody seen my little dog? He's black and white and a bit of a mongrel I'm afraid—'

'Is the dog yours?' said Measle, who had always liked the fact that there was a model dog in the train set. 'I know where he is.'

'Do you think,' said Prudence, eagerly, 'do you think you could spare a very small piece of carrot for him? I'm very fond of Tinker, you see.'

They found Tinker by the street lamp. He was a scruffy little black and white rough-haired terrier, with a stubby tail which stood up straight from his back like a short, furry finger. Feeding him pieces of carrot was difficult. Tinker kept trying to spit them out but they kept on pushing the pieces into his mouth until he was forced to swallow—and, a moment later, he was up on his feet, bounding round them all and barking like crazy.

'That's how Basil caught us,' said Prudence. 'Tinker couldn't help barking whenever he saw Basil. I think he really hates wrathmonks more than I do.'

Lady Grant's shoulders slumped and she stared at the ground in despair.

'Now, now,' said Prudence, briskly. 'Let's not give

up hope. Look at us! We're alive again, thanks to Measle.'

'But how are we going to *stay* alive?' moaned Lady Grant. 'We all know we can't get off the table—it's far too high off the ground. Which means we're stuck here for good. We can't exist on Measle's carrots, can we? I don't suppose there are that many left.'

Measle looked in the paper bag. There were five whole carrots still there, along with several small pieces left over from the chopping process. 'You're right,' he said. 'There aren't many left.'

'Ooohh,' wailed Lady Grant. 'We're all going to starve to death!'

'No,' said Measle, slowly. 'No, I don't think so.'

'Of course we are!' Lady Grant cried. 'We'll be through those carrots in a few days! And then what?'

'Well . . . ' said Measle, shyly, because he wasn't at all sure these grown-ups would think that anything he had to say would be worth much. 'Well . . . surely if a little piece of carrot can bring you all back to life, then couldn't we eat the doughnut crumbs and drink the lemonade and then, when we felt a bit of stiffness starting, we could just swallow a tiny little bit of carrot and we'd be all right again? That way, we could make the carrots last for a really long time, couldn't we?'

Everybody stared at Measle, their faces blank. Measle began to wish he hadn't opened his mouth.

Then Frank smiled. 'Wow,' he said. 'You may be

small but you certainly are bright. We could last a long time with that idea.'

'Yes, very well done, Measle,' said Lady Grant, in her grand voice. 'Such a pity that carrots are so revolting, but I suppose we'll have to make the best of it. Perhaps we might wash them first, though?'

'And we don't need to drink lemonade,' said Measle. 'Basil put in one of those water towers, to fill the boilers of the steam engines. We could drink from that, couldn't we?'

'We certainly could,' said Kip. 'How come you're so clever?'

Everybody gazed admiringly at Measle and Measle felt his face going red. He wasn't used to being thought clever. Basil always made a point of telling him how stupid he was and, until now, Measle had believed him. And it *had* been pretty stupid to think he could get away with playing with the train set—and yet, here were all these good people telling him that he was clever. And, the fact was, (although Measle didn't know it) Measle *was* pretty clever, with a quick brain and a head crammed with ideas all bursting to come out. There was one thought already bothering him and he decided to set it free.

'I'm sorry,' he said, 'but there's something I don't understand. Frank told me not to eat the doughnut crumbs or drink the lemonade. Surely, you all told each other the same thing, didn't you? I mean, while you could still talk?'

'We did,' said Frank.

'Then why did you all do it anyway?'

'Starvation,' said Frank. 'It does funny things to you. You get so hungry, you don't care any more.'

Prudence said, 'I'm told it happens to people when their ship sinks and they're left in a lifeboat with no water. They know that drinking sea water will kill them, but most of them eventually do it anyway. Same story here.'

Everybody nodded gloomily. Then Kip looked up at the distant rafters. 'It's time we got under cover,' he said. 'It's almost dark.'

They all stared fearfully up at the rafters. Prudence said, 'Oh my. I'd forgotten. It didn't bother us when we were plastic, but now—'

'Now, we're in danger again,' said Kip, gathering up his tool bag. 'We'd better get out of here.'

'But where?' said Prudence.

For some reason, they all looked at Measle, as if they were expecting him to come up with the answer. Since Measle didn't yet know what it was that they were frightened of—and since he didn't know the best place to hide—he shrugged his shoulders and looked at the ground, hoping that they would get the answer from somebody else.

'Somewhere strong,' said Lady Grant, decisively. 'Somewhere well-built. I think I know just the place.' She pointed across the town, towards the square. 'I used to hide in the Town Hall—well, it was the only building in this revolting place that even *faintly* resembled my own house, you see. Anyway, I know the structure is pretty sound. It's got a good roof and the walls are solid. I don't think it can get at us in there.'

'What's "it"?' asked Measle, nervously.

Kitty Webb began to cry softly. Tinker, who had been sitting quietly next to Prudence, got up and trotted over to the girl. He peered into her face and then swiped his tongue over her cheeks and Kitty found herself smiling through her tears. Tinker (who thought human tears were just another taste treat) tried another lick. *Nice an' salty, these bits of water,* he thought to himself, *keep 'em comin', little girl!*— but Prudence clucked her tongue and pushed Tinker away gently. She put her arm around Kitty and said, 'It didn't get you before, because you were very good at hiding. We all were. And we're going to go on being good at hiding, aren't we? I think Lady Grant's suggestion is a very good one. I hid there myself quite often and it never got to me, did it?'

Kitty sniffed and wiped her nose on the sleeve of her Brownie uniform. 'But it got some of the others, didn't it?' she said.

'That's because they weren't as quick as we were,' said Prudence. 'And that's why Kip is right. We ought to get under cover, in plenty of time. Come along, everybody. Let's hurry.'

Measle wondered why nobody had answered his question. He decided to ask again, later. In the meantime, he followed the rest of the group as they walked quickly through the darkening streets. Soon they reached the square. As they passed the statue, he turned to Prudence Peyser.

'Do you know what that bit means?' he asked, pointing to the second row of words that were carved into the stone base.

'I do, indeed,' said Prudence. 'The great Roman leader, Julius Caesar, said it when he conquered Gaul. "*Veni, Vidi, Vici*." It's Latin. It means, "I came, I saw, I conquered." '

'Oh,' said Measle.

'A very vain wrathmonk, is our Mr Tramplebone,' said Prudence. 'Imagine—comparing himself to Julius Caesar!'

Measle felt a small tug on his hand. He looked down. Kitty was pulling at his arm.

'Come on,' she said. 'Everybody's waiting.'

Measle looked towards the Town Hall. The rest of the group were already on the steps that led to the massive double front doors and Measle saw Kip and Frank waving urgently in his direction. He turned to Prudence and said, 'We ought to go.'

Prudence looked up at the gathering shadows and then back to Measle and Kitty. 'Yes, yes. Quickly now. There's not a moment to lose.'

She grabbed Measle's free hand and the three of them trotted across the sandpaper grass, up the steps of the Town Hall and through the dark opening of the great doors.

THE THING

The Town Hall had something in common with the long, low railway shed near the coal heap. Of course, it was much bigger and, from the outside, appeared to have three storeys. But, inside, it was the same as the shed—completely empty, just a large, square space with a high ceiling and a bare, new-looking plywood floor.

The group picked a corner to settle down in. William sat down on his suitcase. Frank put his electrician's toolbox down by the wall. Kip stood watching them, his heavy carpenter's bag dangling from one massive hand and his chainsaw and the red fuel can from the other.

'It strikes me that we're quite a useful little crowd,' he said. 'Here we've got a professional electrician, another fellow with a lot of great books, I'm a carpenter and a pretty good one, we've got a lady who knows about wrathmonks—'

'Just a bit,' said Prudence, modestly.

'Well, more than the rest of us,' said Kip. 'Plus—and it's a *big* plus—we've got somebody with a cool head and a quick brain—'

'You're too kind,' murmured Lady Grant.

Kip laughed. 'No disrespect, Lady Grant—but I was talking about young Measle here.'

'Oh,' said Lady Grant. 'Well, of course he's very clever. And sweet. And brave. And very dirty, and with a haircut that defies description—but, nevertheless, we all owe him a vote of thanks.'

Measle felt his face going red again. It seemed to be doing that a lot lately.

Kip said, 'We do indeed, Lady Grant. Thank you for reminding us of it. And last but not least, we have a young lady who—if she's wearing the right uniform—knows a lot about a whole bunch of things.'

So far, Measle thought, little Kitty Webb only seemed to know how to cry. She also seemed to know how to stick herself very close to him—she was there now, right by his side. Measle realized that she hadn't left it since the moment they had revived her.

Kip said, 'Yes. A pretty useful bunch. Maybe we could put our talents together. Do something about getting out of here.'

Lady Grant sighed. 'It's a nice thought,' she said. 'But let's face facts. We're two centimetres tall, we're stuck on a table top with no way of getting down from it, at the complete mercy of that terrible, *revolting* thing in the rafters—'

Measle couldn't contain himself any longer.

'What *is* the thing in the rafters?' he said, so loudly that Lady Grant stopped talking immediately. She, along with all the others, looked at Measle for a moment, as if wondering whether or not to tell him.

Frank said, 'We don't like to talk about it, Measle. But I guess you'd better know. You're going to find out sooner or later anyway.' He stared at Measle, his face serious. 'The thing in the rafters is a bat.'

A *bat*? Measle frowned, puzzled. Bats weren't scary at all—at least, not to Measle. They were just cute little furry things that flew about, eating insects and hanging upside down when they were asleep, looking like Basil's umbrella.

Frank saw Measle's frown. 'Yes, I know. What's so scary about a bat? Nothing—unless you're two centimetres tall. Then they're very scary things indeed.'

'Horrid, revolting things,' said Lady Grant. 'No matter what size you are.'

'And this one is not a normal bat,' said Prudence. 'It's certainly not like any bat I've ever seen.'

'Nothing like it mentioned in my encyclopedias,' said William.

'This one has legs,' said Kip. 'With talons on the end of them. Like an eagle's. No bat I ever saw had talons.'

'Ordinary bats snatch their prey with their mouths,' said William. 'This one grabs its prey with its great, curved claws and then carries it away. Up into the rafters. A very nasty piece of work, I don't mind telling you. Dear, oh, dear, yes. Even worse than my boss.'

Kitty began to cry again. She did it very quietly, burying her face in Measle's sleeve. 'It comes out at night,' she whispered, her voice muffled, so that only Measle heard her. 'It comes out at night and eats us.'

'It didn't eat *you*,' said Measle, hoping that Kitty would stop crying. She was making his shirt sleeve damp.

'It ate lots of the others,' said Kitty.

Measle looked at the group of people. They all had very serious faces and some of them were staring at the floor.

Measle said, 'There were *others*?'

'About twenty,' said Frank. 'All sorts of people, from all walks of life. They were the unlucky ones. They got caught by the thing when they were still human—before the plastic took them over.'

'You see, once you're plastic, the thing doesn't bother with you,' said Kip. 'It can't eat plastic.'

'Meantime—while you're still human—you hide,' said William.

Measle thought about this for a moment. Then he said, 'But you were all *outside* when Frank and I found you. So was Frank, when I found *him*. You weren't under cover—so how come the bat didn't get you when you were still human?'

Lady Grant said, 'We *were* under cover. All of us, most of the time. Especially at night, of course. Particularly as we felt ourselves getting stiffer and stiffer. But, once we were unable to move at all, then that revolting Tramplebone dragged us out of our hiding places with a gigantic pair of tweezers. He very nearly ruined this suit of mine. It's a Chanel, you know—handmade and quite expensive. One simply cannot pull it around the way he did and then expect it to look nice. Anyway, once he'd got us out, he simply placed us wherever he felt like.'

'Look,' said Frank, quietly. He was pointing towards the window. It was dark outside.

'That thing will be coming out soon,' said William. He'd made a kind of chair from his encyclopedias, using two small piles of the books to fashion a pair of armrests for himself, and he was sitting in the contraption, looking comfortable. Measle noticed that the location William had chosen for himself was as far from the windows of the Town Hall as possible.

'I think I want to see it,' said Measle. 'I want to see the bat.'

'OK,' said Frank. 'You'll be safe if you squat down by the window.'

'Aren't you going to watch for it too?' said Measle, hoping for some companionship.

'I've seen it,' said Frank. 'Too many times. We all have, Measle.'

Measle went to one of the tall windows and sat down, his nose just reaching the windowsill. He peered out at the gloom. He could still see the statue in the town square—and the trees that surrounded it—but the houses on the other side of the square were lost in the gathering darkness.

For the first time in a very long while, Measle felt despair creeping over him. His life up until now had been pretty miserable, but Measle was not the sort of person to feel sorry for himself. But now, the future seemed very bleak. He wondered how long they could all survive like this? Not long, surely? A few weeks at most, before the sparse number of carrots he had left in the paper bag ran out. And then what? Starvation, followed by a few desperate meals of doughnuts and pink lemonade —and then the creeping paralysis, with them all ending up like the big carpenter, Kip Lovell. Eventually, Measle reasoned, the plastic would take over completely and there would be no more breathing—which meant, he supposed, death. If you couldn't breathe, you died. It was unthinkable —there had to be a way out of this terrible situation—

Then, he heard it. A distant flapping—not of wings, which make a soft, feathery sort of sound—

no, this flapping noise was different; there was something hard about the sound, as though the wings of this flying creature were made, not of soft feathers, but of some kind of stiff leather. There was a distinct *crack-crack-crack* as it came nearer and Measle thought he could hear a whooshing sound as the wings beat through the air.

Then there was a shape, high above the town. Even at this distance, Measle could see it was big. He could just make out the wings of the creature, batting back and forth as it circled above the buildings. They were wide and black and menacing —*crack-crack-crack*—and Measle saw that, as the thing flew in wide circles, it was steadily descending towards the square.

'It's here,' he said.

There was no reply from the other side of the room. Measle turned his head and saw that everybody in the group was pressed against the far wall, their eyes wide with fear.

'It can't get in here, can it?' he asked.

'I don't think so,' said Lady Grant. Measle could hear the terror in her voice. 'I've hidden here lots of times and I'm sure it knew I was here,' she said.

Measle turned back to the window, lowering his head so that only his eyes showed over the sill. The bat was making one last, low-level circle of the square. It was huge. Now Measle could see the black fur on its underside. He caught a glimpse of the enormous ears, tilted forward and moving from left to right, as the creature strained to listen for its prey. Then, with a sudden flurry of wing beats, it landed in the square. For a moment, it was still. And then it began to move across the square, towards the Town Hall.

The way it moved was so alien that Measle closed his eyes for a second, hoping he hadn't seen what he'd seen. Normal bats, he knew, have a difficult time moving on land. They have to lie flat and pull themselves along with the little claws on their wings. Not this bat—if it *was* a bat. This creature stood on a pair of scaly legs and it walked on them, like a huge bird. There was a scraping sound as its massive talons dragged across the sandpaper grass, then a sudden clattering noise as a great claw knocked the Bengal tiger to one side. The tiger rolled over several times and then crashed into the base of the statue. The bat took no notice. It came on, its head jerking back and forth, like a walking pigeon.

It was getting close to Measle's window. He lowered his head even further, until only one eye was still peeking over the edge. There was a strong smell now, too—like the smell of a mouse cage that hasn't been cleaned in a long time.

The bat loomed huge against the window. Its head was taller than the roof of the Town Hall and it had to bend its body low to put its face to the glass. The enormous head filled the whole space and the eyes—blood red and slanting upwards at the corners—were the size of dinner plates. Its nose looked like a pig's snout, except it was in the shape of a triangular leaf. The tip of the nose wriggled like a pig's and, below the nose, there was a wide, lipless mouth—slightly open, so that Measle could see two rows of needle-sharp, yellow teeth. Its breath steamed up the glass on the outside, but through the fog on the window Measle could see that its eyes—just a couple of metres away from where he crouched—were not looking at him. They seemed to be peering into the room, darting this way and that, never focusing on anything in particular.

Tinker barked. Somebody screamed. At first, Measle thought it was Kitty. He turned quickly and saw that the sharp sound of fear had come from Lady Grant. Her hand was over her mouth and her eyes were wide and staring with terror.

'Sh!' whispered Measle, fiercely. 'It'll hear us!'

'It's heard us already,' hissed Kip. 'Its ears are amazing. It can hear our hearts beating.'

'Don't let it get me,' muttered Lady Grant, through her fingers.

There was a noise behind Measle and he turned back to the window. *Scritch-scritch-scritch*. One of the bat's long claws was scraping down the glass of the window.

'It's getting in!' yelled William, jerking his arms so violently that the two armrests of his book chair spilled to the floor with a thud.

Lady Grant screamed again.

Scritch-scritch-scritch—

Measle saw, to his horror, that the glass was bending under the pressure from the great claw. He scrambled backwards on all fours, until he reached the group that were huddled against the far wall.

'It can smell us, too,' whispered Frank. 'So many of us, all in one place. And no longer made of plastic. It can't believe its luck.'

They waited, holding their breath—

The bending pane of glass cracked with the sound of a pistol shot.

And then, light suddenly flooded the darkness. It wasn't sunlight, which has a hard, bright, white quality to it; this light was a yellowish colour and was far less penetrating—but it was enough for the bat to turn its hideous face away from the window and, a moment later, they saw it back away from the front of the building in a hurried, scrambling sort of way. It seemed to crouch for a second. Then, it sprang into the air. They could hear the *crack-crack-crack* of its leathery wings receding into the distance.

Everybody breathed a sigh of relief and Kitty, who had crawled as close to Measle as she could, said in a small voice, 'Has it gone?'

'Looks like it,' said Measle. 'But where's that light coming from?'

'It's the overhead bulb,' said Frank. 'The one that hangs down from the ceiling, over the train set.'

'More trouble,' said Kip, in a low voice.

'Out of the frying pan, into the fire,' said William.

'It's Basil,' said Prudence, nervously pushing a lock of grey hair off her forehead. 'He's here. And he's going to wonder where we all are.'

They waited, listening to the long silence. Then came Basil's voice, like a thunderclap, directly overhead.

'WHAT IS THISSS?'

It was so loud that a little dust that had collected on the ceiling of the Town Hall was shaken free by the vibration and drifted slowly down through the still air.

'WHAT HAS BEEN GOING ON HERE? WHERE ARE MY SSSPECIAL LITTLE VICTIMS?'

There was another pause and then Basil's voice again, quieter this time—a kind of vicious whisper which sounded like wind whistling in a chimney.

'Thisss is your doing, isssn't it, Measle? You've found all my special little plasticated victims and you've hidden them sssomewhere, haven't you? Now . . . where could you have hidden them? And why? There's a question for you—why would you do sssuch a thing? I want my little victims back where they belong, Measle—ssso, why don't you come out of your hiding place and tell me where you've put them? I won't hurt you, Measle—not if you're quick. Come along, now—show yourself.'

'What should I do?' whispered Measle.

'Stay put,' muttered Frank. 'He doesn't know where you are, and he's not going to tear his beloved train set apart to find you.'

'I wonder about sssomething,' hissed Basil's voice. 'I wonder why—when I came in and ssswitched on the light—why my little furry friend jussst happened to be peering in through the windows of the Town Hall? Why would Cuddlebug be doing that, do you sssuppose? That's his name, you know—Cuddlebug. Sssuch a dear little chap. He and I are the very bessst of friends. He keepsss thisss place ssso clean—not a living thing in sssight! Could it be that Cuddlebug knows sssomething that I don't? Could it be that there's sssomething *hiding* in the Town Hall? Sssomething that Cuddlebug would like to eat? Hmmm? Well, I shall have to get my torch, won't I? I shall have to shine it into the Town Hall and sssee what there is to be ssseen.'

They heard Basil moving away. Measle knew where the torch was. It hung on a hook, right beside the attic door.

'He's going to be back in a second!' he said urgently. 'What are we going to do?'

'He mustn't know we're alive,' said Prudence. 'There's no telling what he'd do to us.'

'Quick, everybody!' said Frank. 'Get into the same positions—the ones we were in when we were plastic! It's our only hope! Measle—try and hide behind us! Come on, everybody, huddle close together!'

Within a few seconds, everybody had crowded together and adopted their statue positions. Lady Grant was crouched huddling on the floor, William was posed as if running for his life, Kitty had her arms wrapped tight round an imaginary pine tree —all positioned as Basil had set them. All except Tinker who, being a dog, couldn't understand what was going on. He whined and pushed his nose against stiff hands, trying to nuzzle everybody back to life.

'Grab him, Measle!' said Frank. 'Try to keep him quiet!'

Measle took hold of Tinker's collar and pulled him into the narrow space behind the grouped figures. He crouched down, his back to the wall, pulling Tinker down next to him. He put his hand round Tinker's nose and whispered, 'Be quiet now, Tinker. That's a good boy. Not a sound, Tinker.'

The little dog seemed to sense the urgency in Measle's voice and he lay quietly by his side, his head on his paws. He quite liked the smelly kid's hand on his nose. The smelly kid's hand was nice and grubby and smelt very interesting. *A bit too much scent of that nasty orange rooty thing that they'd shoved down his throat earlier—but the rest was very appealin'. Mixture of soot and sweat and friendly boy—and a trace of doughnut in there too—yup, very pleasant indeedydoody...*

They all heard Basil's footsteps, coming closer. They all saw the beam of bright light flashing across the tall windows of the Town Hall. They all heard his voice. 'Now then. Let usss sssee what ssso interested my little furry friend.'

A blinding light flooded over them and Frank whispered, through clenched teeth, 'Everybody be still! Not a twitch from anybody!'

There was a gap of about half a centimetre between Lady Grant and William, and Measle could see the window through the little space. He was in deep shadow and felt sure that Basil wouldn't be able to catch sight of him, so he felt safe in peering through the narrow gap. He kept a firm hand on Tinker's nose. He saw the torch sweeping across the window—then he saw Basil's enormous eye next to it.

'Well, well, well,' hissed Basil. 'There they are. One, two, three, four, five, sssix. All present and correct. No—I'm missstaken. Where is the little dog? And where is young Measle? What a puzzle it is, to be sure. All my tiny victims—but no dog and no Measle. Perhaps you've been eaten, Measle? Is that it? Did my furry friend get you? Did Cuddlebug carry you off to his lair in the rafters? Hmmm—on sssecond thoughts, I think not. Not you, Measle. No—you're far too crafty for that, aren't you? Ssso, where are you? And where's the dog? Are you together, perhaps? Are you hiding sssomewhere else, with a plassstic dog for a companion? How sssad, Measle. You and a little plassstic dog.'

Basil's enormous eye withdrew and, a moment later, the bright beam of the torch disappeared, plunging them back into semi-darkness. Now, there was only the sickly light from the bare, overhead bulb.

Basil's voice, high above them now, boomed, 'Well, we shall look for you tomorrow, Measle. Tomorrow, in daytime, when the light is better. And we shall get our long tweezers and we shall take all my little victims out of the Town Hall and put them back where they belong. And we shall find you, Measle. We shall find you and your plassstic dog and we shall punish you for rearranging my train ssset—because nobody but me is allowed to play with my train ssset, Measle. Nobody but me. *In* it, yesss. *With* it, no. Goodnight—and sssleep tight.'

Basil sniggered. Then there was the thud, thud, thud of Basil's heavy footsteps moving towards the door. A *click* of a switch and the yellow light disappeared—followed by the distinct thump as the attic door was closed. Everybody was still. Only when they heard the distant sound of Basil moving down the attic staircase did they drop their posed positions and relax.

'We've got a problem,' said Frank. 'A worse problem than we had before. We've got to hide young Measle, so that Basil can't find him. In fact, we've *all* got to hide—we can't keep up the statue act, not in broad daylight—but Measle has to hide most of all. We need him and there's no telling what that wrathmonk would do to him.'

Lady Grant sniffed. 'But there's nowhere to hide. You know that. I mean, it's a big table, certainly— but that revolting Tramplebone could examine every inch of it in a few minutes.'

'Besides,' said William, 'we can't leave this place. Not at night. Not with that thing on the hunt for us. And my books can't help with a thing like that.'

'There's nowhere for us to go,' whimpered Lady Grant.

There was a long, gloomy silence. Then Kitty whispered in Measle's ear. 'We could be like termites.'

'What?' said Measle.

'Termites. You hardly ever see termites.'

'What was that, dear?' said Prudence.

Kitty looked at Measle, as though she was asking him to explain to the rest of them.

'She said something about termites,' muttered Measle.

'Termites?' said Lady Grant, sounding irritable. 'What is the dear girl talking about? What are termites?'

'Ah well, now—according to the encyclopedia, they're a kind of ant,' said William, in the sort of voice people use when they've learned something by heart. 'Their main diet is wood. In the process of eating it, they can produce extensive burrows. They live in large colonies. There is a queen, who lays eggs—'

'Oh,' said Kip, slowly. 'Now, there's an idea.'

'*What* idea?' said Lady Grant. 'What are we talking about *ants* for?'

Kip smiled. 'Not ants. *Termites*. Termites burrow. They make tunnels in wood—long, twisting tunnels, which keep them safe, out of sight—out of harm's way. I should know—I've seen enough evidence of them in my line of work.'

'How horrid for you,' said Lady Grant, crossly. 'But what have they got to do with us?'

'Everything,' said Kip. He turned to Kitty. 'You're a very clever girl.'

THE TUNNEL

They dug all night.

It was hard going, cutting through the layers of plywood and it would have been impossible without the tools that Kip and Frank had in their kits. Both men had saws and drills and chisels and Kip the carpenter also had the chainsaw, which speeded up the tunnelling enormously. Both men lent spare tools to William and he cut and drilled and chiselled beside them, as best he could.

The idea was to burrow down into the plywood, cutting first a pit, big enough so that even the largest among them could fit into it. Then, they would begin to dig sideways, carving out a horizontal tunnel. At first, there was nothing for Measle, Kitty, Lady Grant, and Prudence to do. But soon, a pile of woodchips had grown by the side of the excavation and the question arose—where to put the debris?

'Basil's sure to see that,' said Kip. Sweat was running down his face.

'We shall have to hide it somewhere,' said Prudence. 'But where?'

They looked around the big room. There was no place that wasn't visible through the tall windows—except, perhaps, for a narrow section immediately beneath the windowsills.

'If we spread the stuff along the wall here,' said Kip, 'there's a chance that he won't be able to see it without removing the whole building—and I don't think he'll do that.'

Now, Measle, Kitty, Prudence, and Lady Grant had something to do. They collected armfuls of the debris and scattered it carefully along the wall beneath the windows of the room. At first, Lady Grant carefully brushed the sawdust off her Chanel suit between every trip but she soon gave that up and hardly complained at all.

Kip had started the process by cutting, with his thinnest saw, through the top layer of a square piece of plywood. He'd chosen a section of flooring in the furthest corner from the door and windows and his saw cut was so fine that, when the piece was replaced, it was hard to see where the cut was. Then, he used an iron crowbar to lever the thin sliver of wood off the floor. This was to be their trapdoor. Once that was done, all three men began to saw and drill and chisel their way downwards.

It took most of the night before the pit was dug deep enough to allow them to start the horizontal tunnel, and the pile of debris that Measle and his helpers had cleared away was almost up to the bottom of the windowsills.

Frank was standing in the pit. His head just reached level with the top. He stopped drilling for a moment and said, 'How thick is this plywood, Kip?'

'Three centimetres. Why?'

'Well, if we're two centimetres tall—most of us, anyway—then that means there's only a centimetre left under our feet. It seems to me that it might be an idea to keep going, until we break through.'

'Break through?' said William, doubtfully. 'We could all fall to nasty, sticky deaths.'

Frank shook his head. 'Not if we're careful, William. My idea is this: if we could cut a small hole down at the bottom of this pit—and make sure it wasn't so big so that somebody could fall through —then we'd have a way of disposing of the rest of the debris.'

'I think you've got something there,' said Kip. 'We're so far from the ground that the stuff is sure to disperse on the way down. I don't think it would form much of a heap, so Basil may not notice anything.'

They attacked the wood and, twenty minutes later, Kip said, 'Hold it. We're there.'

He sent the other two men out of the pit and then, carefully, he chiselled out a small hole. Looking down through the hole made him dizzy. The floor of the attic seemed hundreds, even thousands, of metres beneath him. He gathered some wood chips and dropped them through the small opening, watching them drift down through the still air and noticing, with satisfaction, that they scattered over the distant floor below, so as to be almost unnoticeable.

'Well, it works,' he called and everybody clustered round the top of the tunnel to look down at the hole. 'Now, we can start work on the tunnel. We'll make regular holes in the bottom, just like this one. That way, we can get rid of the chips and get breathing air at the same time. Come on, everybody—back to work.'

Sometime, during the early hours of the morning, Measle heard the *crack-crack-crack* of the great bat's wings as it flew overhead.

'It's come back from hunting,' said Prudence.

'Back from where?'

'From the outside. It checks out the attic first and eats anything that moves. That's why there aren't any insects up here. Then it flies out through the broken window and comes back shortly before dawn.' Prudence looked at her watch. 'There you are—it's five o'clock in the morning. It'll be light soon.'

'Where is it now?' asked Measle, nervously.

'Back in its roost up in the rafters. It'll sleep now until night comes again.'

Prudence went to the pit and called down into it. 'It's almost dawn, boys. How are you doing?'

William popped his head out of the tunnel. He was covered in sawdust and wood chips and he looked very tired. 'Not bad for an encyclopedia salesman,' he said. 'Come and have a look.'

Measle went first, dropping down into the pit. William moved to one side and Measle peered into the tunnel. He could see Kip and Frank at the far end, still chipping and drilling and sawing at the wooden surface. The tunnel was about seven centimetres long, which was more than enough room for all of them.

'That's brilliant,' said Measle, meaning it.

Prudence climbed down, with the help of William. 'How long before Basil comes back?' she asked.

'He always sleeps pretty late,' said Measle. 'I reckon we're safe until nine o'clock.'

William looked at his watch. 'Another four hours. We can dig a lot deeper in four hours.'

The three men kept going. As soon as it was light, Measle, Lady Grant, Prudence, and Kitty went out in search of food and drink. Measle led them to the spot near the railway yards, where he'd found Frank, and they stuffed Lady Grant's handbag with doughnut crumbs. Lady Grant started to tell them that her handbag was extremely expensive, having been handmade for her by an exclusive firm in Rome, Italy, and that perhaps doughnut crumbs were not the most appropriate objects to stuff into such a costly creation, but Prudence cut her short by saying, 'Now come along, dear—there isn't time for all that.'

Lady Grant went a little pink and closed her mouth and said nothing more. She followed meekly as they walked quickly along the railway tracks to the water tower.

Frank had given Measle a plastic bucket and Measle climbed up the ladder on the side of the tower and dipped the bucket into the water. He passed it down to Prudence, and then climbed back down himself.

'This should last us a while,' said Prudence.

They hurried back to the Town Hall. Inside, the men were taking a break. All three were hot and dusty and very thirsty—and they drank the water and ate the doughnut crumbs with gratitude. When they had finished, Measle took the smallest piece of carrot from the paper bag and cut four little chips from it and gave one to each man.

'I hope this works,' said William, swallowing his carrot chip in one gulp.

Frank said, 'It's eight thirty. We ought to hide now, just to be on the safe side.'

One by one, the group dropped down into the pit. Kip went last, bringing a protesting Tinker with him. He pulled the sheet of plywood over his head, fitting it exactly over the gaping hole. 'Let's hope Basil doesn't notice the cut,' he said.

Frank said, 'That's as fine a cut as I've ever seen. And remember, it's pretty dark inside the Town Hall, even with Basil's torch. I don't think he'll see a thing.'

Measle had expected complete darkness in the pit once the cover had been put in place but the little hole at the bottom of the pit let in a small amount of light, so they were able to see the tunnel entrance. They all crawled into the rough burrow. It was now eight centimetres long—more than enough room for all of them, so long as they stayed lying down. There was another small hole drilled into the floor of the tunnel, near the spot where it ended, and the light from this allowed them to see each other clearly.

'What now?' said Lady Grant.

'Now, we wait,' said Frank.

They didn't have to wait long. Soon, they heard Basil's heavy tread coming up the attic stairs; then the creak of the attic door; then Basil's booming voice, muffled now by the centimetre of plywood over their heads.

'Good morning, Measle. I trussst you ssslept well? I have my tweezers, dear boy. Once I've replaced my ssspecial little victims, I shall come looking for you. And, when I find you, I think I shall turn you into sssomething even more unpleasant than what you are now—a dirty, disssobedient little creature. An insssect, perhaps? Yesss—a nasssty, dirty insssect.'

Measle shivered and Prudence put her arm around his shoulders. 'Don't listen to him,' she whispered. 'He won't do anything to you. We shan't let him.'

Measle didn't see how they could stop Basil doing whatever he wanted—but it was kind of Prudence to pretend that they could. He remembered something that she'd said the day before—and a tiny seed of an idea began to germinate in his brain. He kept quiet, because the idea wasn't yet fully formed in his mind—

The roar shook their tunnel.

'WHAT IS THISSS? WHAT IS GOING ON? WHERE ARE THEY ALL?'

The roar became a low rumble of rage— but through the anger in Basil's voice, Measle thought he detected a slight tone of uneasiness, as though Basil, for the first time in his mad and evil life, had met with something he couldn't understand.

'Oh, Measle—you wicked, wicked

boy. What have you done with my little plassstic victims? Where have you put them, eh? And why? Well, we shall find them, make no missstake about that. They can't have gone far, can they? Not with legs as ssstiff as theirs. And neither can you. And, when I find you, yesss—definitely an insssect. A cockroach, perhapsss.'

They heard Basil moving slowly round the great table. Sometimes the wood that surrounded them creaked, as Basil leant his great weight on it and, once, their tunnel shook, as though in an earthquake, when Basil bumped the edge of the table with his hip. Then they heard the thump of his footsteps returning.

'Very clever, Measle. Mossst ingeniousss. I confess—I've looked everywhere and my victims are nowhere to be ssseen. Not on the table, not on the floor. Ssso—what have you done with them? And all by yourssself, too. Mossst impressive, Measle. And now, I am very angry. Very angry indeed. And do you know what I do when I am very angry indeed? I don't get hot, like some angry people do. No—I get very cold. As cold as ice. Like thisss.'

Measle shivered again—but, this time, not from fear. There was an icy chill coming up through the hole in the tunnel floor. He looked at the others, huddled in the dim light and he saw that their breath was coming out of their mouths in clouds of steam.

'What's happening?' whispered Lady Grant.

'It's Basil,' said Prudence, her teeth beginning to chatter. 'He's making it cold.'

'We can't survive this for long,' said Frank, bundling his blue coat around him. 'We'll freeze to death.'

Kip said, 'If it's this cold in here, it's a lot colder out there. Wood is a great insulator.'

'I don't feel very insulated,' said William. 'My bones are beginning to ache.'

Tinker whined softly. He could feel a film of ice forming on his wet nose—*and that was no good, no good at all! How was he expected to smell anyfink with a rotten great iceberg on his snout?* He shuffled round and pushed his nose against Measle's jacket. *Ah, that was better—but now his toes were beginnin' to freeze!* He tucked his stumpy legs under his body and huddled closer to the smelly kid.

Measle could feel little Kitty shivering next to him and he wondered if her tears would turn to ice. Then, a moment later, the cold began to decrease. The icy wind, whistling up through the hole, began to slacken off and, soon, the temperature was back to normal. Then Basil's voice boomed out again.

'Cold enough for you, was it, Measle? Well, tomorrow, it will be much colder. That was jussst a tassste of what's to come, Measle. Tomorrow, it will be ten times colder—and for much, much longer.

At the end, you'll be frozen sssolid, like an ice cube. And that means you'll be dead, Measle. Unless, of course, I find all my little victims back where they belong. Then I won't freeze you sssolid, Measle. No, I shall jussst turn you into a nasssty little cockroach and you can ssscuttle about the table top for as long as you like. Or, at least, for as long as Cuddlebug will let you. Which will it be, Measle? Death by freezing—or life as a cockroach? I know which one I would choose. There's a sssaying, Measle: "When there's life, there's hope". Choose wisely. Ssso—until tomorrow, Measle.'

There was the familiar *thump, thump, thump* as Basil moved away to the attic door. A creak—and then the sound of the door closing, followed by the *thump, thump, thump* as Basil descended the attic stairs.

For a long time, everybody sat in silence. Then Measle said, 'I'm sorry.'

'What for?' said Prudence.

'About all this. Putting you all in danger.'

'Measle,' said Frank, putting both his hands on Measle's shoulders. 'There's nothing to be sorry about. Basil's right about one thing. When there's life, there's hope. You brought us back to life, and that means you gave us hope.'

'And we've got twenty-four hours to think of something,' said Kip.

'What if we plug up the holes?' asked William. 'You said wood is a good insulator.'

Kip shook his head. 'It's good, but not that good. Not against that kind of cold. And remember, this plywood is only three centimetres thick—and we've tunnelled a lot of that thickness away. Now, there's less than a centimetre above and below us —it won't hold the cold away for long.'

'And, if we plug up the holes, we'll run out of air pretty fast,' said Frank.

'What I don't understand,' said Lady Grant, 'is why that revolting creature didn't freeze us all solid there and then? Why wait until tomorrow?'

'I'm fairly sure,' said Prudence, slowly, 'that Basil can only do one major spell every twenty-four hours. It takes a lot of energy to do a major spell like that freezing one.'

'You know about the spells?' asked Frank. 'Do you know how he does them?'

'Heavens, no,' said Prudence. 'And it's all theory, really. But, from my observations of wizards and warlocks and wrathmonks, it does seem that there's a limit to their abilities. Big spells, like chilling a whole room down to sub-zero temperatures—well, they take some doing. Besides, Basil wants us all back where he put us and he wants Measle to do it—and Measle can't do it if he's frozen, can he?'

Measle was thinking hard. The idea he'd had a few minutes before was growing fast. What if, somehow, a wrathmonk's spell could be made to change direction? If, somehow, it could be turned back on itself?

Measle took a deep breath. Then he said, 'I think we should let Basil turn me into a cockroach.'

'What?' said Lady Grant, her mouth dropping open in astonishment. 'Why on earth would we want to let him do that?'

'No, Measle,' said Frank. 'No—we can't let that happen to you.'

'Besides,' said Lady Grant, with a shudder, 'I hate cockroaches. Ugly, smelly, revolting things.'

Measle shook his head. He turned to Prudence and said, 'Look, if you're right, there's a good chance he won't succeed. It's risky, but it might just work—and, anyway, there's nothing else we can do.'

Then he told them his idea.

STRIKING
Back

It wasn't a long walk to the little house by the lake. It took them ten minutes to reach it.

The house—it was more of a cabin, really—stood deep in the shadow of the trees that surrounded it. It was made of logs and was small — once inside, there was little room to move around. There was one advantage it had over the Town Hall: there was only one tiny window, far too small for the bat to get through. The cabin also appeared to be well-built and they felt pretty sure that it could withstand any number of attacks from the monster—if it ever discovered they were inside.

Once they had made camp in the cabin, Measle led the way to the lake. It was nothing more than a mirror, cleverly cut in a random shape so as to resemble a small body of water set deep in the forest. It was fixed into the plywood surface of the table and surrounded by low banks of green-painted sandpaper, which looked remarkably like grass.

Kip, Frank, and William set to work. Using crowbars from the tool kits, they began to loosen the mirror from its setting, being careful all the while not to crack the thin glass. It took a long time, pushing the bladed ends of the crowbars under the lip of the glass, bit by bit, and gently easing it out of its setting. Shortly before it got dark, Kip and Frank gave one last heave and, with a crackling sound, they lifted one edge of the mirror, tilting the whole thing up at a narrow angle. Then the rest of them, except for Measle, ran forward and took hold of a section of the mirror.

'All right,' shouted Kip. 'All together now! Lift!'

Everybody strained their muscles and one side of the mirror lifted clear from its setting—a whole half a centimetre.

It was enough. Measle quickly crawled forward and fitted his thin body in the narrow gap between the underside of the mirror and the plywood table top. Tinker, thinking this was some new kind of game, crawled in beside him and Measle gently pushed him away. 'No, Tinker,' he said. 'Go away, there's a good dog.'

Then he crawled backwards onto the sandpaper bank and, with a collective sigh of relief, the rest of the group lowered the mirror back in place.

'Well, it ought to work,' said Frank.

'But it's a terrible risk, Measle dear,' said Prudence. 'Remember, it's only a theory. It could all go badly wrong.'

Measle grinned at her, pretending to be brave. He was, in fact, very frightened by his idea—but it seemed that there was nothing else they could try. He busied himself helping the men to cut some short lengths of wood. Kip cut down a small tree with his chainsaw and they chopped the trunk into centimetre pieces. Then they took the sections of timber to the lake side. Once again, the men levered the mirror up. Once again, Lady Grant and Prudence joined in, to hold the side of the mirror clear, while Measle and Kitty propped the lengths of wood under the glass. Once they'd set the first three in place, Kip said, 'OK—lower away.'

Slowly, gently, they lowered the mirror onto the props. Then they set the remaining sections of timber around the edge of the glass, until Kip was satisfied that the thing was steady and firm.

'Do you think Basil will notice?' asked Prudence.

'He'd have to look pretty close to see it's not flat,' said Kip.

'Let's hope he doesn't look close,' said William.

'Let's hope he'll be looking at me,' said Measle.

'Oh dear,' said Prudence. 'I do worry about this.'

They returned to the cabin, just as the light from the broken attic window began to fade. They all went inside the cramped area, closed the door and settled down on the floor.

William said, 'I've had a tiny thought. To match my tiny brain.' He turned to Prudence and Lady Grant. 'Do either of you two ladies have any perfume in your handbags?'

Prudence shook her head. 'Never use the stuff.'

Lady Grant said, 'I've got some. Why?'

'I want to try something,' said William. 'I want to mask our smells with something else. I read in my books that, if you make yourself smell of something else, then animals that rely on their sense of smell sometimes get confused. It seems to me that, if we spray ourselves—and this room— with some good, strong perfume, then perhaps the bat might leave us alone.'

'It's worth a try,' said Frank.

Lady Grant rummaged in her handbag and pulled out a small square bottle, with a spray cap. She dusted some doughnut crumbs off it and said, 'This is very expensive. It's called *Jolie Femme*. It's my favourite scent. I do hope you're not going to use all of it?'

William smiled. 'Lady Grant,' he said, 'if we ever get out of this mess, I'll buy you a case of the stuff.'

Lady Grant smiled faintly. 'That is terribly sweet of you,' she murmured. 'But I'm afraid you wouldn't be able to afford a whole case. I don't know *anybody*—except me, of course—who could afford a whole case.'

William grinned and took the bottle and began spraying everything in the room—the walls, the little window, the door, and Tinker, who sneezed and wiped his eyes with his paws. *That's the kind of stink*—he thought to himself—*that a self-respectin' dog can do without, thank you very much!*

Next, William used what was left in the bottle to spray everybody's clothes—Measle most of all, because Measle seemed to have the strongest smell of all of them.

'You ever hear of a bathtub, kiddo?' he said, grinning, as he squirted Measle's dirty old shirt.

'Have you ever seen my bathtub?' said Measle, wrinkling his nose against the strong scent. 'If you had, then you wouldn't take a bath either.'

Soon, the darkness came and, with it, the *crack, crack, crack* of the great bat wings. They heard it flying over the cabin, the sound getting closer and closer. Then there was a thump as the bat landed—and a rustling noise as it pushed its way through the trees.

'It's coming,' whispered Kitty.

They all huddled together, holding their breath.

There was a snuffling sound, right outside the door—then, in quick succession, three short, sharp sneezes. A moment later, they heard a sudden whoosh of wind and then *crack, crack, crack* as the bat took off.

'It didn't like that,' said Frank. 'Good idea, William.'

'Yes, a *very* good idea, Mr Durham,' said Lady Grant. 'A rather *expensive* idea—but a very good one all the same.'

'With any luck, it won't be back,' said Frank.

They slept that night, some more soundly than others. Measle lay awake for most of the hours of darkness, thinking about the next day. It wasn't very comforting, the three fates that lay ahead. Death by freezing. A short life as a cockroach. Or, with a great deal of luck, the one remaining possibility—

He fell asleep at last, an hour before dawn. A moment later (or so it seemed) Frank shook him awake.

'It's time, Measle. Are you sure you want to go through with this?'

Measle nodded. He wasn't sure at all, but he knew he had no choice. Prudence hugged him, Lady Grant kissed the air somewhere near his cheek, and Kitty began to cry. The three men solemnly shook his hand.

'However this comes out, Measle,' said Frank, 'we want you to know that we think a lot of you.'

'You're a brave kid,' said Kip.

'Knock 'em dead,' said William.

Measle gulped. Suddenly, it seemed like a terrible idea. He looked round at all the worried faces. They were relying on him. This was no time to back down.

'OK,' he said, his voice strong. 'Here I go.'

He walked out of the cabin and heard the door close behind him. He made his way through the trees to the edge of the mirror lake. It was just as they'd left it the night before—tilted up on one edge, leaving a gap of half a centimetre between it and the plywood base. Measle tried to imagine how it would look from above. The angle of the tilt was very small—with luck, Basil wouldn't notice it.

He sat down on the sandpaper bank to wait. He felt very lonely and very nervous—and horribly exposed. A whole mob of butterflies seemed to be having a party in his stomach and his mouth felt as dry as dust.

The seconds ticked by—then the minutes— then a whole hour had come and gone, and still no Basil. Measle began to hope that perhaps he'd never come. Perhaps he'd decided to leave the house for ever? Perhaps he'd conveniently died in his sleep? Perhaps he'd—

Thump, thump, thump. Basil was coming up the stairs. Measle stood up, trembling. His knees started to knock together and he felt suddenly weak. He forced his unwilling legs to take him to the edge of the mirror, so that his hips were pressed against it—and he looked towards the distant door, waiting for the terror that was approaching.

The door opened and Basil was there—huge and towering, his white face whiter than usual, his eyes more staring than ever, and strands of his lank, greasy black hair hanging over his high white forehead as if—in his hurry to get his revenge—he'd forgotten to use a comb. Measle watched as Basil walked slowly to the edge of the table. He stood quite still, waiting for Basil to see him.

And then Basil did see him. His great round eyes narrowed and he smiled his terrible smile. He moved round the table, to the point closest to Measle, and he leaned both his waxy hands on the surface and lowered his massive head.

'Ssso—there you are, Measle. Taking a little ssstroll in the woods, are we? Fresh air and exercise—ssso good for the lungs, aren't they? Now—let me try to remember—what were we going to do with you? Ah, yesss—we were going to freeze you sssolid, weren't we?'

Measle blinked. *What about the other spell— the cockroach threat?* He thought as fast as he'd ever thought.

'I don't care if you freeze me solid!' he shouted. 'Just don't turn me into a cockroach!'

'*Don't* turn you into a cockroach? What do you mean "*don't*"? We don't sssay "*don't*" to Basil, surely?'

'I don't care what you do to me—just, please, *please* don't turn me into a cockroach!'

'There's that "*don't*" again, Measle.'

'And I mean it!' shouted Measle, at the top of his lungs. 'Don't, don't, *don't* turn me into a cockroach!'

'Ah—ssso, that's what we fear the mossst, is it?'

'Yes! I couldn't bear being a cockroach!'

'Very well, dear boy. Then—a cockroach it shall be! Ssstand quite ssstill, Measle.'

Even through his fear, Measle couldn't help feeling a small satisfaction at the success of his ruse and it occurred to him that, perhaps, Basil's madness had a shrinking effect on his intelligence. Basil leaned forward on his hands and lowered his head closer to where Measle was standing. Then, he narrowed his round fish eyes. Measle tensed, concentrating on Basil's dark pupils. The moment he saw the glint of green fire in those fishy orbs, he dived—in one smooth movement—under the tilted mirror.

Basil followed the sudden, unexpected movement of the boy and, at the precise moment when the twin beams of green light flashed from his eyes, he found himself looking directly into the reflecting surface of the mirror. The lime green rays hit the mirror and bounced—at the speed of light—right back into Basil's eyes. He screamed— whether from pain or fear, Measle didn't know—and there was the sound of sizzling, like

bacon frying in a hot pan. Measle huddled under the edge of the mirror. Something was happening out there—but what?

The sizzling noise stopped.

Silence—then an odd scrabbling, clicking sort of sound, coming from a long way away. Measle cautiously crawled out from beneath the mirror and looked up. Basil had gone—disappeared. It was as though he'd never been there and all was quiet—apart from the scrabbling, clicking sound in the distance.

There were too many trees between Measle and the noise. There was only one way to find out what was making it: Measle picked a nearby pine tree, with lots of strong branches at regular intervals all the way up the trunk. He began to climb it. It was lucky he'd chosen a tall one—quite near the top, he found himself looking out over the canopy of the forest. He could see all the way to the edge of the table—and what he saw made his blood run cold.

There, far in the distance, clinging to the edge of the table with its two front legs, was a gigantic, jet black cockroach. It was at least ten centimetres long. Its antennae were waving frantically and it was trying desperately to heave the rest of its body up onto the table. As Measle watched in horror, the creature made one last effort and slowly pulled its huge body over the edge. Once it was safe, on level ground, it paused for a moment, its antennae waving back and forth, as if it was getting its bearings. Then, it turned in Measle's direction and began to move slowly across the table top towards him.

Measle shinned down the pine tree as fast as he could. When he reached the bottom, he raced back to the cabin and threw open the door.

'Quick, everybody! We've got to get out of here! It's coming!'

'What's coming?' said Frank. 'Did it work?'

Measle gasped, 'It worked OK. It worked really well. That's the trouble. Come on! There's no time to lose!'

'Where are we going now?' said Lady Grant, not moving from her corner of the cabin.

'We've got to get back to the tunnel!' shouted Measle. 'It's the only safe place, now! Come *on*!'

'But I prefer it here,' said Lady Grant, still not moving.

'Better do as Measle says,' said Frank. 'And, looking at his face, we'd better do it fast.'

There was such authority in Frank's voice that everybody got to their feet without another word. Together, they crowded out of the cabin and, with Measle leading the way, they began to run through the forest. Frank drew level with Measle.

'What are we running from, Measle?' he panted.

Measle, panting as hard as Frank, told him. Frank nodded, then, turning his head to the others, he shouted, 'As fast as we can, everybody!'

They made it with only millimetres to spare. The giant insect was delayed momentarily by the thick forest between it and the cabin, but it skirted the trees and headed fast towards the town. Measle and the rest of them raced through the trees, burst out of the wood and made for the outskirts of the town. As the group neared the buildings, they could hear scrabbling footsteps close behind them. Nobody dared to look backwards—the sound of the creature was terrifying enough to keep them all running as fast as they could. They tore along the empty streets, with Prudence huffing and puffing in the rear. At one point, she stumbled and almost fell—but Kip put out one big hand and steadied her. Too tired to speak, Prudence nodded her thanks and they ran on, dodging round corners, their breath rasping in their throats. At last they reached the square, with the Town Hall on the far side. They dodged past a small group of plastic townspeople, then on past the statue, hearing the clicking, scrabbling noise coming closer and closer. Measle glanced back— and saw the cockroach just turning the corner. He saw the creature barge straight through the group of plastic figures, sending them flying right and left. It grabbed one of the figures in its jaws—the figure was of a boy, about Measle's age and size— and with a crunch the great jaws slammed together. The cockroach shook the whole front section of its body, like a wet dog emerging from a bath—and the two halves of the plastic boy flew to either side of the monster, the neatly cut sections skittering and sliding across the sandpaper grass.

Measle gulped in horror. It was as if the cockroach had meant to demonstrate its power to Measle and had chosen the figure of a boy of Measle's stature to drive the point fully home. It seemed to be saying, *That's what I shall do to you—when I catch you, Measle!*

'Come on, Measle!' screamed Frank and Measle turned away from the terrible sight and raced for the Town Hall. At the great open doors, friendly hands grabbed him and pulled him into the safety of the room—then those same hands heaved the doors shut with a bang.

'What is that revolting thing?' panted Lady Grant, staring in horror through the tall window at the approaching monster.

'That's Basil,' gasped Measle. 'And he's really, *really* angry.'

'Come on, everybody,' said Frank, herding them all towards the pit in the corner of the room. 'It's not safe out here. We've got to get into the tunnel.'

They hurried down into the pit, just as the giant cockroach reached the front door of the Town Hall. They crawled into the tunnel and huddled together at the far end.

'What happened back there?' said Frank, when he'd caught his breath.

'Basil was leaning on the table,' said Measle. 'So he didn't end up on the floor like we'd hoped. When the spell got directed back at him, I think his hands turned into insect claws and he managed to hang on to the edge of the table and then pull himself up.' He looked around at the frightened faces. 'I'm sorry—I guess we're in even worse trouble now.'

'I don't think so,' wheezed Prudence. 'I'd rather have to deal with an oversize insect than with Basil.'

'Me too,' said William. 'Apart from anything else, there's the size difference. A ten centimetre cockroach is bad—but a full-size Basil is worse. As bad as my boss.'

'At least we know that your theory was right,' Frank said, smiling at Prudence.

Prudence didn't look happy. 'I've just remembered something,' she said, quietly. 'You see, there's a second part to that theory.'

'A second part?' said Frank.

'Yes. It's generally believed that a spell that's turned back on itself loses a certain amount of power.'

'It doesn't seem to have lost anything,' said Frank. 'Basil tried to turn Measle into a cockroach, and now he's one himself. I think it worked fine. Of course, it's much bigger than we'd hoped—'

'It's not the effectiveness of the spell that's changed,' said Prudence, shaking her head. 'It's the duration. A weakened spell has a time limit. Twenty-four hours—or so it's believed—and then the thing wears off.'

'Well, OK,' said Frank, smiling. 'That gives us some time to come up with something—'

Then he stopped smiling—because, overhead, there was the sound of wood splintering, and plaster crumbling, and bricks falling—

'What's happening now?' said Lady Grant. There was a trace of panic in her voice.

'I think it just pushed its way into the Town Hall,' said Frank.

'Like a bulldozer,' said William. 'A battering ram.'

'It can't get at us, can it?' said Lady Grant.

'I don't think so,' said Kip. 'Plywood is strong stuff.'

There was the sound of something scraping over the floor above their heads. Then, a shaft of light appeared at the end of the tunnel.

'It's pulled away my trapdoor,' said Kip.

A shadow fell over the pit. Then a long, black, bristly, stick-like object descended into the hole. It moved backwards and forwards, its tip searching for the tunnel entrance—

'What is *that*?' gasped Lady Grant.

'That's one of its legs,' said Frank. 'Everybody—squeeze up tight against the wall!'

They huddled together, pressing themselves against the wall at the tunnel's end. The tip of the leg found the tunnel entrance and began to move slowly towards them, like a huge, hairy snake—and, with it, came the smell. A rancid, bitter smell of cockroach. There was a hooked claw on the end of the leg, and it scraped against the tunnel floor as it advanced.

Kitty screamed.

'It's all right,' said Prudence, putting a motherly arm round the girl's shoulders. 'It can't reach us.'

Measle wished he could believe that. There didn't seem any stopping the thing. The claw came closer and closer, weaving from side to side. Then, when it was only a centimetre from the huddled bodies, it stopped. Slowly, carefully, it explored the sides, the floor, and the ceiling of the tunnel. Then, suddenly, it retreated quickly. As the cockroach pulled its leg out of the tunnel, it scraped it hard against the corner, where the tunnel met the pit, and a shower of wood splinters fell from the roof.

'That was too close for comfort,' said Frank.

'You're right,' said Kip. 'We've got to dig some more.'

The three men attacked the wooden face of the wall with every tool they had and soon there was a growing pile of wood chips and sawdust on the floor. Measle, Prudence, and Kitty pushed it all through the nearest hole. Lady Grant did nothing to help them; she just stared with wide eyes towards the pit at the far end of the tunnel.

They dug for hours, lengthening the passage by a few centimetres.

'That'll do for the moment,' said Kip, his face streaming with sweat and his hair grey from sawdust.

'We'd better cut another hole in the floor,' said Frank. 'We're going to need all the air we can get.'

Cutting down through the remaining half centimetre of plywood took another five minutes. It was Kip who broke through and he widened the hole until it was big enough.

'Hey—look at this,' he said, peering down at the opening he'd made.

'What is it?' said Frank.

'Looks like an electric cable. But you're the expert, Frank. You tell me.'

Kip moved aside to let Frank take a look.

'You're right,' said Frank. 'That's one of mine. I think it's the main power line that connects the control centre to the tracks. I reckon I can reach it.' He lay down and pushed his arm through the hole. 'Yup. It's right under us.'

Kip tapped him on the shoulder. 'You say it leads to the control box?' he said.

'Yup. Right up inside.'

'And it's made of steel? The control box?'

'Yup. It's a steel box, screwed down into the plywood.'

Kip thought for a moment. Then he looked sombrely round at the group. 'I think that's where we ought to be,' he said. 'Inside a steel box. Nothing— not the bat or the roach—can get at us there.'

'All this running about. Surely we're safe enough here?' said Lady Grant, not taking her eyes off the far end of the tunnel.

As she spoke, the black leg appeared again in the pit. This time, it made no effort to approach them. Instead, it manoeuvred its hooked claw to the angle where the tunnel and the pit met. The claw dug deep into the tunnel ceiling and then pulled hard. It strained for a moment—and then there was a splintering sound as a section of the tunnel ceiling was ripped away. The claw withdrew, dragging the ragged piece of plywood with it. A moment later, it reappeared. Once again, the claw dug into the roof of the tunnel, strained, and then yanked another section away.

'It's trying to dig us out,' said Frank. 'I didn't know roaches were so clever.'

'That's no ordinary cockroach, Frank,' said Prudence. 'Basil's brain is in there, remember? He may be mad, but he can still think.'

Kip took Lady Grant's small, smooth hands in his huge, rough, black ones and stared into her face. 'Still believe we're safe enough here?' he said, quietly.

'No, Mr Lovell,' whispered Lady Grant. 'No, I don't.'

They dug downwards, enlarging the hole at their feet and trying to ignore the sounds of splintering wood behind them. The cable was directly beneath them, perhaps two centimetres below the level of the bottom of the hole. When the hole was big enough, Frank said, 'I installed it —I guess I get the right to go first?'

There was no argument. Frank lowered himself into the hole, until only his head and shoulders were showing. 'Got it,' he said. 'I'm touching it with my toes. If you men could grab my hands and lower me down a little further—'

Kip and William took hold of Frank's arms and slowly let him down further into the hole.

'OK—I'm standing on it now,' said Frank. 'You can let me go. I'm going to drop down on my hands and knees.'

Kip and William let go of Frank's hands and Frank disappeared from view. 'It's good,' he called. 'Let me have the kids next.'

William and Kip lifted Measle into the hole and slowly lowered him. Measle felt his ankles grabbed from below and then Frank's reassuring voice. 'I got you—you're almost there—just a little bit further.'

Measle's toes touched down on a solid surface and, a moment later, he was lying face down on a curved section of black rubber. Frank was kneeling beside him. He said, 'Whatever you do, Measle, just don't look down. You're safe if you don't look down.'

Measle looked down. He couldn't help it—his curiosity overcame his fear and he turned his head and looked over the edge of the cable. Then he brought his head back quickly and closed his eyes. The floor was so far away and his position on the rounded top of the cable seemed so precarious that he felt suddenly dizzy. He dug his fingers into the hard black rubber surface and pressed his body as flat as it would go.

'Crawl along a little way, Measle,' said Frank. 'We've got to make room for the others.'

Slowly, Measle inched himself forward along the cable. He knew, logically, that if he was careful, there was little danger of his falling. The cable was thick and strong and as wide as a double bed— but the fact that it curved away downwards on

either side of him was very disturbing and he was careful to stay in the exact centre of the cable— and equally careful to hold on very tight.

It took some doing—and a lot of terrified squealing from Lady Grant—but eventually everybody was lying prone along the cable. Prudence stuffed Tinker into the front of her old anorak and did up the zip, so that only his head was protruding. Kip was the last to lower himself down the hole and join them. He brought with him both tool kits and his chainsaw, all hanging from his broad leather belt. 'Stupid to leave them behind,' he said. 'We might need them again. OK, Frank, lead the way.'

Frank looked back over his shoulder. 'Everybody take hold of the person's ankle in front of you and go really slowly.'

They inched along the wire that stretched over the dizzying drop. Behind them, the sound of splintering wood grew fainter as they put distance between it and themselves. The underside of the table was close above their heads and, as they moved forward, it gradually got closer and closer —until Measle could feel the smooth plywood scraping on his back. In front of him, Frank stopped.

'Hold it,' he said. 'There's a staple up ahead. I remember putting it in to stop the cable from dangling. We've got to get round it somehow.'

Measle lifted his head and peered over Frank's body. Just in front of Frank, the cable was fixed tight to the underside of the table with a steel staple. There seemed to be no way of getting past it. Frank crawled forward, his head bumping on the ceiling. Measle watched as Frank reached forward and grabbed the side of the staple. Then he did a very brave thing: he let his body slide to one side, so that he was hanging by his hands, his chest and thighs dangling against the curved side of the cable.

'Oh—do be careful, Mr Hunter,' called Prudence, from somewhere behind Measle.

Frank grunted. Then he began to swing his body from side to side. Each swing was wider than the last until, with one huge effort, he managed to pivot his legs past the staple and back up onto the cable on the far side. Still holding tight to the steel bar, he pulled the rest of his body up until he was once again lying flat on the curved rubber surface.

'OK—here's what we're going to do,' he called. 'I'm going to help each one of you past this thing. You've just got to trust me—I won't let go. Kip—if you could come up to the front and help me with the heavier ones? Measle—you first. Grab my hand.'

The dizzy feeling swept over Measle again and, for a moment, he couldn't move. 'Come on, Measle,' said Frank, quietly. 'Any kid who can do what you did out there by the lake can do this. Give me your hand.'

Measle took a deep, shuddering breath and reached out his hand. He felt the cold metal of the staple—and then Frank's strong grip on his wrist. 'Good boy,' said Frank. 'Now, just let yourself slide sideways. Don't worry—I've got you.'

Measle swallowed hard, took another deep breath, closed his eyes and then shuffled his body to the right. He felt himself slipping over the edge

—but Frank's grip on his wrist was like a bracelet of iron and, even as he started to slide down the curved surface of the cable, he felt himself being pulled upwards. He kept his eyes tight shut, until he was sure he was back on solid rubber—then, cautiously, he opened them. Frank was grinning at him.

'There—that wasn't so bad, was it?'

Kitty came next. Measle noticed that she seemed to have little fear and never closed her eyes for a second. She even smiled when she was dangling from Frank's hands and seemed almost to enjoy the whole experience which Measle had found so frightening.

'Weren't you scared?' he whispered, when she crawled next to him.

Kitty pointed to a badge on her uniform. 'It's a climbing badge,' she said. 'I've always been good at climbing.'

One by one they all made it past the staple. Lady Grant screamed several times and Prudence (who was carrying the added weight of Tinker) had to be swung past the obstacle by both Frank and Kip, both men holding tight to her wrists—but neither she nor Tinker made any fuss at all and soon she was sitting safely on the other side of the staple, patting her grey hair back into place.

Kip was the last to come over and he needed no help—even with the heavy tool kits dangling from his belt. He imitated Frank and swung himself past the obstacle, using his great strength to haul himself up to safety.

Ahead of them, the cable looped down at a shallow angle and then looped up again, disappearing in the distance through a neat, circular hole cut in the plywood ceiling. The party dragged themselves forward, each person clutching the ankle of the one in front of them. It took them a long time and, when they at last reached the opening, they were all tired. On the final stretch, the upwards slope of the cable meant that they had to pull themselves hand over hand, hauling themselves up the long black rubber hill until their arms ached with the effort. Prudence was the most exhausted of all of them and Kip, bringing up the rear, had to push against her feet to help her up the incline.

At last, they made it. One by one, they crawled up through the round hole and, once safely inside, they dropped off the cable and stood thankfully on solid ground.

The inside of the control box was a strange place. It was dark, apart from a few narrow beams of light that streamed through a wide mesh grille on one wall. Everywhere there were wires—in different colours—running to connections over their heads. There was the smell of oil and a faint scent of ozone in the still air. Kip knocked on one wall. 'Solid steel,' he said. 'Nothing can get in here.'

Lady Grant sat dejectedly in a corner, her head

in her hands. 'But we can't stay in here for ever,' she moaned. 'We'll starve to death.'

'We have to get rid of the roach,' said Frank. 'We have to get it off the table somehow.'

'Wait a minute,' said William. 'Won't the bat do that for us? Tonight, when it's out hunting? I bet that cockroach would make a great catch for it.'

Frank had been peering out through the steel grille. He said, 'Come and take a look—we've got a grandstand view from here.'

They all clustered round the grille. Through the narrow bars, they could see, in the distance, the roof of the Town Hall and the tops of the trees in the square.

'If anything happens tonight,' said Frank, 'between the bat and the roach, I mean, we'll see it. I'll take the first watch.'

THE STEEL BOX

That night, once again, the bat came flapping in great circles over the table top. *Crack, crack, crack* went its wide leather wings. The group, woken from fitful sleep by the sound, pressed their faces against the grille. They could see the bat's huge shadow against the pale walls of the attic. They watched as it wheeled over the great table and they saw it suddenly check its flight, seeming to hover for a moment, before it dived straight for the Town Hall.

'It's seen the cockroach,' said Frank.

The Town Hall was shrouded in darkness and anyway, at this distance, they were unable to see what was going on. But they could hear—and what they heard was very strange. A great cacophony came from the town square—a screeching and a scratching and a rattling and an odd, and very unpleasant, high-pitched hissing, that seemed to go on for several minutes.

'What's happening?' said Lady Grant. 'Why doesn't it just grab the revolting thing and fly away?'

The reason the bat didn't simply take hold of the giant cockroach was this: inside the insect's brain were remnants of Basil's mind—and Basil was no fool, which made the cockroach that he'd become a lot smarter than the average cockroach. For the first time in his long and evil life, Basil was afraid—and what he feared was his own little pet, Cuddlebug. He knew that Cuddlebug would never recognize his master under the black, shiny carapace of the cockroach. He knew that Cuddlebug would merely think he'd found the finest and largest meal of his life. So Basil the cockroach had to find shelter. He'd smashed his way into the Town Hall, ramming his huge body through the centre doors and bringing down most of the front wall and a good part of the ceiling with it. Even with this destruction, there was enough left of the Town Hall to shield him from the bat's talons and, by turning his hard, shell-covered wing cases towards the shattered front of the building, Basil presented to his attacker a smooth, solid, and unbreakable surface, which the bat—scratching and clawing as hard as it could—was unable to get hold of. The curved talons scraped and slid over the unyielding surface and, all the time, Basil the cockroach kept his body pressed hard against the back wall of the room, clinging on with his claws and never budging an inch. And all the while, he kept up a steady, high-pitched hissing sound, which—to the listeners inside the steel box of the control centre—was the only noise that they were unable to identify.

'What's going on over there?' said William.

'Sounds like a fight of some sort,' said Kip. 'I think the bat is having problems.'

Then there was silence. They stared through the grille, straining their eyes in the darkness. A moment later, they heard the *whoosh* as the bat took off and the *crack, crack, crack* of its wings fading into the distance as it flew towards the broken window at the far end of the attic.

'Did it get it?' Prudence asked.

'Let's hope so,' said William.

Then, far away, they heard a shuffling, scraping sound, as if some great creature was shifting its body into a different position.

'I think I spoke too soon,' said William. 'I don't know how it did it—but I think it beat the bat.'

Kitty was staring at the ceiling of the steel box. She said, 'I bet I could get through that.'

The rest of the group looked at her and then followed her gaze upwards. Set into the top of the box was a series of narrow slots and, through them, they could just make out the rafters of the attic high above them.

'You silly girl,' said Lady Grant. 'Why would you *want* to get through it?'

'I bet I could see everything from up there.'

'I bet you could,' said William. 'And you're the only one who could squeeze through there, too. I certainly couldn't and that's a fact.'

Prudence shook her grey curls. 'But, my dear— what if it comes for you?'

'Well, I can get back in quickly if it starts coming this way,' said Kitty.

'You're a real little trouper,' said Frank. 'OK—but be careful.'

Kip hoisted Kitty onto his broad shoulders. She

reached out her hands and grasped the bars above her head. Then she stood upright on Kip's shoulders and he took hold of her feet and gently pushed her upwards. Kitty wriggled her shoulders, then the rest of her body, through one of the slots and, a moment later, was standing on the top of the control centre.

'Oh, wow,' they heard her say.

'What can you see?' said Kip.

'Everything,' came back Kitty's voice. 'I can see all over the whole layout from here.'

'What about the town square?'

'Well, it's a bit dark—wait a minute—I can see the front of the building . . . it's all smashed in . . . some of the roof has fallen down . . . but there's something moving in there . . . something big and shiny . . . it's turning round . . . it's coming out— ooh, help!—it's coming this way—'

They saw Kitty's legs dropping down through the slot and Kip stepped forward and grabbed her ankles and lowered her gently to the floor.

'It's the cockroach all right,' Kitty panted. 'It doesn't look like it's hurt at all—and it's headed right here.'

They all heard the sound of its pattering feet drawing closer and closer and they all smelt the cockroach stink as it reached the steel box. Its huge shadow fell across the grille in the wall. Then there was a slithering, rasping sound as it pulled its body up onto the top of the control centre and then its black belly flattened against the ceiling slots.

'It's right on top of us,' whispered William.

'We're safe enough,' said Frank. 'But, to be safer still, let's get under there.'

He pointed to the far wall. Some kind of electrical junction box stuck out from the side of the steel wall there, forming a low cave just beneath it. The group ran across the space and crawled under the ledge—just as one long, hairy, black roach leg squirmed between the ceiling slots. They all pressed themselves tight into the small space. The claw on the end of the leg touched the ground in exactly the spot where they had just been standing—then it scraped slowly across the floor, weaving back and forth, covering every inch of the ground in its search for them. It tapped against the protruding ledge—and then curved round beneath the ledge and began to inch its way towards them.

Lady Grant moaned in terror, pulling her feet away from the approaching horror. As she did so, a shoe slipped off her left foot. Without thinking, she reached forward to snatch it—and Kip grabbed her by the waist and dragged her backwards.

'But—that shoe is a *Manolo*!' whispered Lady Grant. 'Do you have any idea what they *cost*?'

'I don't care if it's a diamond the size of your head, lady!' muttered Kip. 'Stay back!'

The claw scraped over the floor—and then, it

touched the shoe. It strained forward, the whole leg quivering with the effort—and then it hooked the shoe and pulled it back and up and out of sight.

'My lovely Manolo!' wailed Lady Grant.

'At least we know how far it can reach,' said Frank. 'And it can't rip its way in here.'

For the rest of the night, the cockroach stayed pressed against the roof of the control centre. Occasionally, it would push one of its legs through the slots and explore the interior of the box, while the group inside huddled close together under the protective ledge. Towards dawn, it shifted suddenly —sliding with a thump off the steel box and then pattering away towards the town square.

'It knows the bat is coming back,' said Frank. 'It'll head for the Town Hall again.'

Measle crawled out from under the ledge and the rest followed him. They made themselves as comfortable as they could and waited for daylight. Measle couldn't sleep. Another idea was forming in his head. He stared up at the coils of multi-coloured wires that draped and looped around the inside of the box. He didn't know anything about electricity—but there was someone there who did. He went over to Frank, who was leaning against the wall grille, his eyes shut.

'Frank? Are you awake?'

'I am now,' said Frank, opening one eye.

'I was wondering—do you think it's possible to get the power on?'

'What—to the train set?'

'Yes.'

Frank raised one eyebrow. 'What do you want to do that for?'

'I'm not sure,' said Measle, with a shrug of his shoulders. 'But could it be done from inside here?'

Frank gazed up at the wires, his expert eyes flicking round at all the junctions and connections. 'I suppose it could be done,' he said at last. 'It's just a question of re-routing a few lines. See that red cable? We could take a connection off that and then link it up to that black one over there —yeah, it can be done.'

'What about making the trains move?'

'You want the trains to move? Why? Have you had another idea?'

'Well, I might have,' said Measle. 'But it all depends on the trains moving. Could that be done, too?'

Once again, Frank stared up at the lines of electrical cables. He didn't answer for some time and, all the while, his eyes were scanning the wires. At last, he said, 'I think it could. We can't turn the spindles—they're too heavy for us—and those spindles control the train speed. That would mean that the trains would be going full tilt from the start—they'd probably come off the tracks on tight corners—but it's the best we could do.'

'Could you control different trains?'

'Yes. Each one of those yellow wires goes to a different section of the track. All we have to do is patch in a temporary cable from there to there—one for each train—and we got it. So—what's the plan?'

'There's one more thing I need to know,' said Measle. He pointed to the grille, set in the steel wall. 'I'm going to have to get through there.'

Frank examined the narrow bars of the grille and then looked at Measle. 'Well, you're skinny—but not that skinny. Little Kitty might be able to do it, but not you.'

'It has to be me,' said Measle, firmly. 'Could we cut one of the bars?'

'It'll take some time,' said Frank. 'We've got two hacksaws between us, but this bar is pretty thick.'

'But it could be done?'

'Yes, it could be done.' Frank stared hard at Measle. 'But before we start on something that's going to take a good two hours, I'm going to want to know why.'

Measle sat down next to him and outlined his plan. As he did so, Frank's eyes got wider and wider and, when Measle finished, he let out a big sigh and said, 'It's out of the question.'

'Why?'

'Because it's too dangerous, that's why.'

'The mirror thing was dangerous too and you all let me try that.'

Frank shook his head. 'That was different,' he muttered. 'This time, there's a lot more that could go wrong.'

'But you think it might work?'

Frank thought for a moment, his forehead creased in a frown. Then he said, 'It's possible. It's completely crazy—but it's possible. But we can't let you do it. If anybody does it, it ought to be an adult.'

'No,' said Measle, quietly. 'It's got to be me. First of all, it'll take too long to cut enough of the bars to let an adult out—and, second of all, it's me that Basil wants. It's me that he's furious at—not any of you. He just wants all of you back in your proper places. Me, he wants to kill.'

'And that's why we can't let you do it,' said Frank, closing his eyes and leaning his head back against the grille.

'What about if we voted on it?' said Measle.

Frank sighed. 'I guess you're going to tell them, aren't you? And I guess maybe some of them will *want* you to do it. Well, we live in a democracy, I suppose. And a democracy means that everybody gets a say. OK—if you insist. We'll take a vote. But let me tell you right now—I'm going to vote "no".'

The vote was split right down the middle.

Frank, Kitty, and Prudence were strongly against the idea. Kip, William, and Lady Grant were for it. Kip and William were worried by the scheme but they both agreed that there seemed to be no alternative. Lady Grant just moaned and said,

'Anything! Anything to save us from that revolting monster!'

'Looks like we're stuck for a decision,' said Frank. 'You can't go unless there's a clear majority, Measle.'

'Well—what about me?' said Measle. 'Don't I get a vote?'

'Of course he does,' said William. 'It's the democratic way.'

'Well—I vote "yes" too,' said Measle.

'What a surprise,' said Frank, flatly.

There was a lot to do.

Kip and William began the long, tiring process of cutting through one of the bars on the steel grille. Their hacksaws were tiny, compared to the thickness of the metal and, after an hour of solid work, they had only managed to cut halfway through one bar. Meanwhile, Frank was busy on the electrics—cutting through the plastic coating on one, splicing another onto the exposed copper, re-routing a third in a long loop that ran clear across the room—and, all the time, humming softly under his breath as he worked.

Soon after daylight, the sawing work on the steel bar was stopped by a sudden loud buzzing noise, that seemed to come from all around them.

'Power's on,' said Frank. There was the smell of ozone in the air and already they could feel the interior of the box losing its night-time chill. Frank dragged a length of red wire across the floor. 'It could get pretty hot in here,' he said.

It took another hour to cut through the bar and, by the time they were finished, Kip and William were streaming with sweat and William's hands had developed several blisters.

Frank pulled the red cable to one of a row of junction boxes set high on the wall. He took a sharp knife from his toolbox and stripped the plastic sheathing from the end of the wire, exposing the bright copper strands. 'OK,' he said. 'We're ready to go. All I've got to do is touch this cable end to one of these connections and you've got a train. Question is—which one?'

'Time for our lookout,' said Kip. He hoisted Kitty onto his shoulders, lifted her up to the ceiling slots and Kitty wriggled through the bars and onto the roof of the box.

'Where's the cockroach?' Kip called up to her.

'It's in the square. Right up next to the statue. It's not moving. No—wait a minute—it's waving its antenna things.'

'Revolting,' said Lady Grant, who had taken off her remaining shoe and was holding it close to her, as if it were some precious object.

Kip turned to Measle. 'OK. We're all set, Measle. This is it.'

'Please be careful, Measle,' said Prudence.

Kip brought something out from behind his

back. He held it out to Measle. 'I think you might need this,' he said. 'Or rather, *we* might need it. It'll help us to see you.'

Measle took the object and examined it. It was a short length of wood with a small, red, triangular flag nailed to one end.

'See,' said Kip, 'I thought if you could stick one end of that in your belt, we'd have a better chance of pinpointing your position. All we have to do is look for the flag.'

Measle pushed the end of the stick into the back of his trousers and tightened his belt. The flag hung at arm's length over the top of his head.

'Now,' said Kip, 'when you get outside, we should be able to see where you are.'

Everybody seemed to think it was a good idea. Measle thought it was an excellent one—he liked the idea that somebody would be following his progress. Somehow, it made him feel just a little more secure. Frank was the only one who remained silent. Suddenly he stepped forward, frowning.

'I don't want you to do this, Measle. In fact, vote or no vote, I've changed my mind. I'm not going to let you do it. It's just too dangerous.'

There was a long, awkward silence. Then William said, 'Dear, oh, dear. You sound like my boss. I thought this was a democracy?'

Frank nodded curtly. 'It is. But somebody has to make responsible decisions. Measle's just a kid, for God's sake!'

Measle looked round the steel room, staring hopefully into each face for some show of support. But nobody wanted to meet his gaze. Their eyes slid away from his, some looking down at the floor, others peering up at the ceiling—and Kip shook his head sadly and said, 'He's right, you know, Measle. It's too risky. I know I voted to let you go—but I've changed my mind as well.'

William said, 'Yes. There must be another way. Sorry, Measle.'

Kitty sniffed. 'I never wanted you to do it,' she whispered.

Measle looked at Lady Grant. She was sitting close to the wall, her hands limp at her sides, her legs stretched out in front of her. She met his eyes and Measle could see the indecision in her face. They looked at each other quite blankly for several seconds. Then she did a strange thing. She *winked* at him.

There was another long silence, as awkward as the first. Then, suddenly—and without warning— Lady Grant screamed.

'Owwww! Owwww—that hurts! My hand! My hand!'

Everybody stared at her. Her eyes were tightly closed and her whole face was screwed up in a tight grimace of pain. Her right hand was hidden behind her back and, with her left, she was clawing frantically at the air. Prudence hurried over to her and squatted by her side.

'Whatever's the matter, dear?'

'My hand! It's got my hand! Make it let go! Owww! *Owww!*'

Frank took two strides and was by her side. He bent over and grabbed her right arm.

'No! That hurts! Let me go!' shrieked Lady Grant.

Frank pulled again, more gently this time. 'What's got your hand? There's nothing there, Lady Grant. Look—there's nothing there.'

Lady Grant opened her eyes. 'Isn't there? Really? Are you sure? Good heavens, you're right. But I could have sworn that something was biting my hand.'

Frank shook his head. 'Well, there wasn't. Now, I don't know what all this was about but—wait a minute!'

Lady Grant took a deep breath and yelled, 'Now, Measle! *Now!*'

Frank whirled round. 'No!' he shouted.

He was too late. While everybody's attention was elsewhere, Measle had been edging steadily towards the grille and now he stepped up to the gap in the iron bars and, with one fluid movement, he wriggled through.

'Measle! Wait!' shouted Frank, reaching out through the bars.

Kip put his hand on Frank's shoulder. 'Let him

go,' he said, quietly. 'We can't stop him now.'

Frank turned and stared angrily at Lady Grant. 'You shouldn't have done that,' he said quietly. 'That was a bad thing that you did.'

Lady Grant tilted her head to one side and shrugged. 'You won't say that if he saves us,' she said calmly.

Outside the safety of the steel box, Measle felt very alone and very exposed. He walked a little way, until he could no longer hear the rest of the group. Then he turned and looked back. Kitty was standing on the roof of the control centre and she waved at him. Measle, feeling far from brave, waved back.

Inside the box, everybody was so intent on watching Measle through the grille that nobody noticed Tinker until it was too late. The little dog slipped away from Prudence, tore silently towards the grille, jumped with one bound onto Kip's back, over his head and through the hole they had cut. He barked with pleasure at his new-found freedom and raced towards Measle.

'No, Tinker!' whispered Measle. 'Go back!'

Tinker took no notice. He wasn't going back in that strange dark box for anybody, not even for this nice smelly kid who was making shooing movements at him with his hands. He danced happily round Measle, his tongue lolling, his eyes rolling and yelping with joy—and suddenly Measle didn't feel quite so alone any more.

'Come on then, dog,' he said. 'Let's go and do what we've got to do.'

He reached around his back and settled the stick into his waistband. The flag fluttered gently over his head. Then he took a deep breath and began to walk away from the control box.

THE ENGINE

In a wide arc around the control box, the table top had been left bare—but thirty centimetres away from the steel housing the green-painted sandpaper began and, within another fifteen centimetres, there was the start of the forest.

Measle set off across the table top, his heart thumping in his chest. Tinker, seeming to sense the importance of their mission, trotted quietly at his side. They moved, as silently as possible, between the trees, walking roughly in the direction of the town square.

Measle was trying as hard as he could to picture in his mind the entire layout of the train set. He concentrated particularly on the rail line that ran from the dirty railway yard, through the outskirts of town and into the forest. He reckoned that, if he and Tinker kept walking in a straight line, they should come across the tracks fairly soon—and moments later, there they were, gleaming in the morning light. He stepped onto the line and looked left and right. To his left, about sixty centimetres away, the tracks disappeared in a wide turn that Measle knew led back towards town. To his right, the tracks led away in a straight line for several centimetres and Measle could see, in the far distance, the point where they met the very edge of the table. There, the line made a sharp turn to the right and Measle knew that the track ran alongside the edge of the table for most of its length, then, at the table's end, it made another wide arc before doubling back on itself.

'This is where we do it, Tinker,' he said. 'I just hope I can run as fast as you can. Come on.'

They began to walk between the rail lines, stepping on each broad railway sleeper and avoiding the loose gravel that lay between them. Measle tried a short run—yes, it was possible to get quite a good speed up, leaping from sleeper to sleeper—until his foot slipped and he hit the gravel, instantly tripping and falling hard on the sharp stones. He sat there for a moment, pressing his scraped hands to his chest. Tinker stood quietly by his side, with a puzzled look on his face. *Was this part of the plan?* he thought. *Or is it 'cause the nice smelly kid just ain't any good at*

runnin'? Of course, four legs is better than two—
stands to reason, dunnit?

Measle got to his feet, patted Tinker on the head and they began to walk again.

They followed the line as it curved round to the right. On either side, the trees seemed to press in against them and, once they had passed the long bend, Measle was relieved to see the dirty railway yard buildings in the distance. He could just make out the hulking shape of the big black locomotive, its huge cow-catcher sticking out in front like a set of buck teeth. The engine seemed to be crouching, ready to leap forward at a moment's notice.

They walked on for a few more metres and then —as Measle had expected—they came to a point where the forest thinned suddenly on the left hand side of the tracks. Here, Basil had left a broad open area in which he had set the logging camp. Small huts stood on either side of a muddy track. The logging mill itself was set by the side of the tracks and Measle could see the dusty machinery in its gloomy interior. There were the stumps of newly-cut trees everywhere and one even had an axe head embedded deeply into it, its handle sticking up at an angle.

Measle and Tinker left the tracks and set off up the muddy track—which was, of course, not muddy at all. It was perfectly dry, but Basil had scrunched up the sandpaper here and painted it brown, so that it looked like a rutted, potholed pathway through the woods. The track twisted this way and that, but most of the turns were to the right and Measle knew that, quite soon, they would reach the outskirts of the town.

'Can you see him?' Kip called up to Kitty, who was still standing on top of the box.

'I can see his flag,' she called back.

'Where is he now?'

'He's almost at the edge of town—just coming out of the trees, along the dirt road.'

'Good,' called Kip. 'Keep your eyes fastened on that flag.' He turned to Frank, who was standing by the row of connectors, the red cable in his hands. 'Ready?' he said.

Frank nodded. 'As ready as I'll ever be.'

This is the hard part, Measle thought, as he and Tinker cleared the last of the trees and stepped into the edge of the town. *This is the part where luck has to take over.*

The houses here were in the form of small cottages, all stuck together in a line on either side of the street. Each little house had a small front yard and in these areas stood the rubbish bins— two for each house. They were the old-fashioned sort, made of galvanized corrugated steel, with round lids, each with a handle on it. Measle went to the nearest house and took the lids off two of the bins. He held them up like cymbals.

'I'm going make a lot of noise now, Tinker,' he said.

This is it, he said to himself. *It's now or never.*

Measle raised the two steel lids high in the air, separating them as far as his arms could stretch. He swallowed once, gritted his teeth, and then brought his hands together as hard as he could. The steel lids crashed together with a great clanging sound that seemed to bounce off the walls of the cottages, echoing back and forth between the houses.

Tinker dropped to the ground, his stubby tail between his legs. *What was the smelly kid doin'? Oh no—he's doin' it again! Crash! Clang! Smash! Bang!* Well—whatever the smelly kid was doing, it looked as if he was enjoying himself—so Tinker decided that this was all part of some new game. A musical game, perhaps? He jumped to his feet, his tail high. He lifted his head and started to howl—a high-pitched, yodelling yell that mixed horribly with the discordant crashes of the steel lids. *Crash! Howl! Clang! Howl! Smash! Howl! Bash! Howl!*

And, in the town square, the cockroach's antennae turned.

They turned in the direction of the sound.

Basil—or what remained of Basil inside the giant roach—had suffered an unpleasant night. Being an insect was bad enough—but being attacked by his own little pet was an appalling state of affairs. That he'd survived the night at all was due entirely to the fact that he'd managed to control the suicidal tendencies of the body he was inhabiting. There was just enough of Basil's brain—mixed in with the brain of the monster insect—to override the mindless instincts of the cockroach. The creature had wanted to turn and face its attacker—but Basil's superior mind had managed to force it to turn its hard, slippery back to the bat and, at the same time, cling with all the strength in its massive claws to the walls and floor of the half-demolished Town Hall. It was lucky that Cuddlebug also had a reasonable intelligence (for a bat) because, after scrabbling uselessly at the hard wing cases of the cockroach for ten minutes, he had decided that the insect simply wasn't worth all this effort and that there would almost certainly be easier pickings somewhere else. So, as suddenly as it had begun, Cuddlebug had stopped his attack and flown off through the high attic window and into the night outside. And Basil, once again overriding the roach's natural instincts—which were to scuttle about the place looking for scraps of food—had held tight to the wall and floor of the shattered building for a further ten minutes, just in case Cuddlebug had decided to come back and try again. Once it was clear that the bat had gone for good, Basil had scuttled across the table and had spent another frustrating few hours trying in vain to get at that filthy little Measle, together with his little plastic victims who had—and this was the most infuriating and puzzling part of it all—somehow come back to life.

And now, both he and his cockroach host were very, very hungry. Basil was also in a savage fury and this clashing, crashing, banging sound, somewhere at the edge of town, was making his brain ache. Dimly, in his muddled mind, he realized that the noise was almost certainly being made by that horrible boy—for who else was there? His plastic victims somehow were no longer plastic, so it was possible that they were responsible—but, no. Only a dirty, filthy, sneaky boy could be causing such a racket—

Basil turned his great body, so that he faced the direction from which the noise was coming. He waved his long antennae in the air, tasting the scent atoms that blew in the slight breeze—*yesss! It was him! That foul little Measle—he should have disposed of him years ago! Well—he'd dispose of him now! He'd dispose of him and eat him, ssstarting with his head and working his way ssslowly all the way down to his toes! And that would be the end of the filthy creature! Yesss—*

Basil heaved himself forward and, with gathering speed, began to scuttle towards the sound.

Tinker smelt the cockroach long before Measle saw it. The dog suddenly stopped howling and turned his nose in the direction of the town centre. He crouched low, his stubby tail tucked between his hind legs, the wiry hair on his shoulders rising into a stiff crest and a low, rumbling growl sounding deep in his chest.

'What is it, boy?' said Measle, halting his lid-bashing for a moment. Tinker growled again, his nostrils twitching. 'Is it coming?' Measle asked, the pitch of his voice rising through fear. Tinker darted him a quick glance, as if to say, *Of course it's comin'—can't you smell it?*

And then, rounding a corner at the end of the street, came the great black cockroach, its antennae waving furiously and all six legs pumping back and forth as it scuttled towards them—and Measle dropped both steel lids to the ground with a crash and turned and fled, Tinker close behind him.

Inside the control box, all eyes were staring upwards through the ceiling slots.

'What's happening, dear?' asked Prudence.

'I'm not sure,' called back Kitty. 'Could you hear the noise?'

They had all heard it. Tinker's howls and the crashing of the steel lids were way in the distance but they had heard the sounds quite clearly.

'Is there any movement?' called Kip.

'No, not yet—wait! The noise has stopped! Yes! I can see the flag . . . it's starting down the muddy road . . . it's moving fast! And . . . and . . . the cockroach is chasing him!'

'Tell us when he reaches the railway tracks!' shouted Frank.

'Any minute now,' said Kip, quietly.

Frank nodded and moved the hand holding the red cable a little nearer the row of connectors.

Measle and Tinker raced down the wide path. Behind them—and getting steadily nearer—was the pounding, scratching sound of the roach's claws. Sometimes they heard the sound of a tree breaking and falling as the great insect bulldozed its way down the track towards them.

By the time they reached the railway tracks, Measle was panting with exhaustion. Tinker's tongue was lolling out of the corner of his mouth but he looked as if he could run for ever. Behind them, the sounds of pursuit were getting louder. Measle reckoned that the cockroach was just now reaching the far edge of the logging village— which meant that, at its present rate of speed, the monster would be on top of them in fifteen seconds. Measle made a quick decision. He risked five of those precious seconds to reach behind him and grab the stick in his belt. He pulled it clear

and waved
it frantically,
reaching up as far
as he could, the little
red flag fluttering
wildly in the air.

Kitty's voice was a high-pitched scream.

'He's at the tracks! He's waving the flag! The cockroach is—oh, no!—the cockroach is almost there! Wait! Measle's moving again! He's moving fast down the tracks! The cockroach is right behind him!'

'Now!' shouted Kip.

Frank turned and touched the exposed end of the red cable to the first yellow wire. Kip looked back towards the ceiling slot. 'Is there a train moving?' he shouted.

There was a pause—then Kitty called down, her voice desperate. 'It's the wrong one! It's the little freight engine! And it's going *backwards*! Try a different one!'

Kip nodded to Frank and Frank moved the red wire to the next yellow one in line.

'What now?' called Kip.

Another pause—and then Kitty's voice, breaking with panic. 'No! No, not that one! That's the passenger train! And it's on the far end of the table! Do another one!'

Frank touched the cable end to the third wire.

Measle's legs felt like lumps of hot lead. The effort of running across the sleepers—and avoiding the gravel in between them—was enormous. The railway tracks stretched out in front of him, as straight as an arrow to the far table edge. Measle knew that there were, in fact, only a few metres between him and the sharp curve at the end—but it looked like a kilometre at least and he wasn't sure he was going to make it. He pounded on, his heart thumping in his chest, his feet slapping down on each sleeper in turn. Tinker ran beside him, occasionally throwing a look backwards and growling deep in his throat. The sound of breaking trees had stopped—and that meant only one thing: the roach was on the tracks now and, by the steadily increasing volume of its scraping claws against the iron rails, it was gaining on them rapidly.

And Measle knew he wouldn't make it. It was too far to the edge of the table—he was too tired —and where was the expected sound of the great locomotive? It should be moving by now. It should be on the very tracks they were running along. He should be able to hear it. But he could hear nothing, except his own rasping breaths, his feet slap-slapping on the railway sleepers and the terrifying sound of scraping and scrabbling and scratching and hissing—all too close behind him.

Then, out of the corner of his eye, he saw Tinker skid to a stop. He ran on a few paces and then halted himself. He turned—and saw Tinker racing back along the track, straight towards the great insect.

'No!' he yelled. 'Tinker! Come back!'

But Tinker didn't come back. Tinker had had enough. *All this runnin' around and makin' loud noises was all very well—but no self-respectin' dog was goin' to allow himself to be chased by a bug! It may be the size of a house, with huge nasty , dangerous-lookin' fangy thingies in its mouth—but what does that matter? It smells like a bug—an' that makes it a bug! Just a stupid old bug! And I'm a dog—and dogs ain't scared of bugs! It's the other way round, isn't it? And now the smelly kid is yellin' somethin'—prob'ly tellin' me to go for it! Right—I'll go for it! I'll show the smelly kid what I'm made of! Okey-dokey—let's start with the growly-snarly-show-the-old-toothies routine, shall we?*

And Tinker, his lips pulled back in what he hoped looked like the most savage of savage snarls, bunched the muscles of his short back legs and accelerated towards the giant cockroach.

For a moment, faced with the onrushing dog, Basil forgot what he was and felt a moment of fear. He'd always hated dogs. They scared him. Those teeth! That noise they made whenever they saw him! He'd always avoided dogs—apart from this one—and he'd felt nervous all the time it was near him. He'd managed to threaten the old woman when he'd caught her spying on him, telling her to keep the dog away from him or he'd do something really nasty to them both. Once he'd got them inside his house, he'd locked them in a dark and damp cupboard under the stairs and had turned them both tiny by blowing hard through the keyhole. But now here was this full-sized dog racing towards him, snapping and snarling and frothing at the mouth—and Basil stopped, his huge claws skidding across the railway sleepers and crunching against the gravel. Tinker stopped too. He lowered his head and snarled, showing off his white teeth. The cockroach did nothing for a moment—and, a few metres down the track, Measle watched as the dog-sized Tinker and the elephant-sized insect warily stared at each other.

Then Basil remembered what he was. He was a giant cockroach! This tiny creature couldn't hurt him! Its little teeth were no match for his great curved mandibles! Its soft skin couldn't compete with his hard shell! Any damage that was going to be done would be done by him! Basil lunged forward—and Tinker neatly side-stepped the great roach and circled round to its side, barking furiously. Basil heaved his huge body round to face the dog and lunged forward again—and again, Tinker jumped backwards out of reach. Slowly, they circled each other, Basil moving ponderously forward, his curved jaws snapping and Tinker jumping—at the last second—out of reach of the attacks and barking continuously.

In the control box, Frank had almost run out of wires to touch. He'd tried them all and, each time, Kitty—her voice rising with hysteria—had called down that it was the *wrong train*! And now there was only one connector left to try.

'It's got to be this one,' he muttered. 'It's just *got* to be!'

He touched the red cable end to the last of the connectors.

Measle had seen enough. It looked as if Tinker was well able to fend for himself and this was an opportunity to get to where he wanted to be. He turned and ran down the track, towards the distant table edge. Behind him he heard the sound of Tinker's barking—and the cockroach's furious hissing—dwindle as he raced away. Within half a minute, he'd reached his goal. Where the railway tracks met the edge of the table, it made a hard turn to the right—and this would be where he would make his stand. If only the train would come!

He felt it long before he saw it. He was standing near the edge of the vast table, with one foot resting against the left rail. As he watched the distant battle—Tinker still leaping nimbly away from Basil's ponderous attacks, Basil heaving his massive body round to face the dog again—he became aware of a slight tingling vibration in his toes. He looked down. The rail seemed normal—and yet he could feel it distinctly now. A trembling, a faint pulsation, which quivered through his foot, into his ankle and up his leg. He dropped to his knees and put one ear to the cold steel—and there was a thrumming sound in his head that grew steadily louder and louder and louder—and there, far away up the railway tracks, just rounding the gentle curve, came the great black locomotive, its pistons pounding, its wheels a blur, and its massive cow-catcher skimming the rails towards him.

Tinker and the gigantic insect were too busy sparring with each other to notice what was bearing down on them and Measle saw that, unless he did something fast, there was a good chance that Tinker would be hit by the train. He put his fingers in his mouth and blew a piercing whistle —and Tinker jerked his head in Measle's direction.

What's he want, that smelly kid? Can't he see I'm busy here? An' there's that whistlin' noise again! Does that mean he needs me? Maybe it's time to go—this fight's gettin' a bit borin',—an' now there's a funny noise, too—it's gettin' louder an' louder—it's a bit scary, this funny noise—an' now it's gettin' so loud that it's not so funny after all! An' that means—yip! Time to go—

Measle saw Tinker suddenly leave the battle and begin to race towards him, his ears flattened, his legs stretching out in a breakneck gallop—and he saw the giant roach turn as well and begin to scuttle after Tinker, its six legs pumping back and forth as it gathered speed—and behind the roach, gaining on it rapidly, came the great, smoke-belching, wheel-screaming, piston-packing, rail-rattling locomotive—

Measle stood perfectly still. There was nothing left for him to do. Whatever was going to happen would happen now without any interference from him—just as long as the cockroach stayed between the tracks—

Then Tinker, tiring of running across the railway sleepers and scratching his paws on the gravel between them, veered suddenly sideways, running off the tracks and onto the painted grass at the side—and the great cockroach veered away too, off the tracks and out of danger—out of danger from the black, pointed cow-catcher on the front of the huge locomotive—

Measle thought desperately. Then he started to yell, jumping up and down in the middle of the railway lines, waving his red flag as hard as he could, frantically trying to get the roach's attention away from Tinker and onto himself—

—and Basil saw the red flag—and under it the nasty, dirty, leaping figure of the boy—the boy he hated far more than he hated any stupid little dog —The boy was jumping up and down in the middle of the tracks—and Basil forgot about chasing the stupid little dog and changed direction again, scrambling back between the railway lines— and now he was almost there and he could see in his muddled mind's eye how he was going to flatten the filthy boy—flatten him and eat him, starting with the top of his head and working his way to the soles of his feet—he was almost there—

— and just as Basil reared his huge body forward to squash Measle flat, Measle hurled himself to one side, off the railway tracks and onto the painted grass at the side, rolling as he landed and keeping rolling sideways until his body thumped against the trunk of a tree. Basil could never shift direction as fast as that. In a straight line, he could get up a terrific speed but the great mass of his cockroach body could never perform an agile move like Measle's, so he merely slowed down his forward pace and laboriously began the process of shifting his great body sideways.

He was too late.

The massive cow-catcher on the front of the locomotive—skimming a centimetre above the rails—slammed into him, catching his body from underneath and flipping it high in the air. Measle watched as the huge cockroach turned end over end, spinning upwards towards the attic ceiling. He felt the blast of wind as the locomotive, with the three dusty Pullman carriages, shrieked by. He saw the locomotive, going at full speed now, hit the sharp turn, rock violently from side to side, its small front wheels grabbing at the bending rails— and then the entire engine seemed to leap half a metre in the air as it left the tracks, hurtling straight ahead over the edge of the table. He heard the crash as it hit the attic wall—and then three successive crashes as the Pullmans hit as well. He looked up again and saw that Basil's spinning, upward flight was slowing down and that, at any moment, he would begin the inevitable descent back towards the table top—and Measle saw, with a sudden flash of horror, that Basil wouldn't fall over the edge of the table as he'd hoped he would —no, the cow-catcher had flipped Basil straight up in the air and not sideways at all, which meant that Basil would land back on the table top—and Measle knew that, no matter how high you dropped a cockroach, their hard outer shell always protected them from harm—

High in the rafters, Cuddlebug stirred. There was so much *noise* down there. Far more noise than usual. Crashing and smashing and bashing. This noise was very disturbing to a bat's sleep. Very disturbing indeed. So disturbing in fact, that—

Cuddlebug opened one eye.

And here was lunch.

It was very strange. Lunch had never come to him before. He always had to seek lunch out. *Find* lunch. *Catch* lunch. And only then, *eat* lunch. And yet, here was lunch, spinning up towards his roost in a very peculiar flight pattern indeed—and it looked just like that large, juicy cockroach that had given him such trouble only a few hours ago—and who knew that cockroaches could fly? And since when did a bat eat its lunch in broad daylight? And who cared? Opportunities like this were rare—

Lazily, Cuddlebug reached out one enormous talon and grabbed Basil neatly out of the air.

And then the cockroach spell wore off.

It didn't happen all at once. The only evidence that the spell had run its course was that the cockroach, held firmly in Cuddlebug's grasp, began to get heavier. The bat's first reaction was, *Ooh, great! A fatter lunch!* But then the weight began to be a burden—and Basil's insect body started to swell, so that Cuddlebug's talon began to ache under the strain of holding it—and then the weight became so much that the bat's other talon, which was holding fast to the beam above it, began to slip away—and then Cuddlebug lost his grip on the beam entirely and together, he and Basil began to fall towards the table top. Instinctively the bat spread its great leather wings, which turned its downward fall into a glide—but lunch was getting too heavy and too fat and it was somehow changing shape in Cuddlebug's grasp, so Cuddlebug brought his other talon into play and now grasped the body with both sets of claws— *yes, he had a better grip now*—but his glide path was dropping fast and he made a wide circle over the table top, looking for somewhere that would give him much needed height again—*ah! The open attic window! If he could only get through there in time, before gravity completely overcame him!* The bat flapped its great wings frantically and flew fast towards the broken window, gaining just enough height to clear, by a centimetre, the shards of dirty glass that stuck up from the base of the window frame like jagged spears. Out into the open air Cuddlebug shot— *and, oh! The daylight! Too bright! His eyes! He was blind! Which way to turn?*—and, in his confusion and sudden blindness, Cuddlebug forgot everything he ever knew about flying and lunch and the effects of gravity—and as Basil's insect body grew and stretched and softened and changed its shape back into its human form, Cuddlebug, flapping furiously in crazy circles, suddenly lost his battle with the pull of gravity and began to plummet towards the distant ground.

Instinctively, Cuddlebug opened his claws and released his burden.

And in that moment, Basil was Basil again. He felt the sudden slackening of the grip—the grip of his beloved pet that had carried him safely, until this very instant, through the air—he felt the wind whistling past his face—he glimpsed the ground rushing up to meet him—

Basil had instincts too.

Basil's instinct was to grab at something—anything!—just so long as it would stop this headlong plunge—and he grabbed and clung tightly to the only objects within his reach. To the talons that had just let him go.

And Cuddlebug shrieked a batty shriek of fear and fury and flapped his great leather wings as hard and as fast as he could. But it was no use. Gravity was winning this battle—and winning it in a spectacular fashion.

It was a long way from the attic window to the hard concrete pavement far below. And Basil, now fully re-formed back to his wrathmonk self, no longer had his hard outer cockroach shell to protect him. And Cuddlebug had always been soft —on the outside, at least.

Measle saw none of this—but he could hear it all. From somewhere beyond the attic window, he heard three sounds. Cuddlebug's shriek of terror was at too high a pitch for human ears to hear, so the first sound to reach Measle's ears was Basil's long, howling scream as he plummeted to earth. The other two came a moment later. One loud, the other soft. Both were squishy—

SPLAT! And then, a second later—splat!

Measle closed his eyes. His back hurt from where he'd rolled against the tree. He lay still for a moment. Then he felt something wet on his face—something wet and warm. He opened his eyes. Tinker was crouching over him, licking his face.

Tinker was getting bigger.

THE FALL OF THE HOUSE OF TRAMPLEBONE

Measle could see that Tinker was getting bigger because of the way that the surrounding scenery seemed to be shrinking. Where, moments before, the nearby trees had loomed large over the dog, now Tinker was half their height. His body now straddled all the way across the railway tracks, which seemed to be getting smaller and smaller— and yet, Tinker didn't seem to be getting bigger in relation to *him*. Which meant—

He was growing too.

He glanced about him. Yes! His head was now higher than the trees; he could look out over the forest; he could see the entire table top—and over there, the control box looked as if it was lifting itself clear off the surface of the table. He watched as the screws holding the box down on the plywood sheets were wrenched out of their holes with the sound of tearing wood—and then, with a pop, the box was thrown to one side and he could see a very squashed-looking group of people crawling out of its shadow. And they were growing! Growing fast! And now his own arm brushed against the forest and thirty trees were demolished! He sat up quickly and felt the table wobble beneath him—he heard the creak as his weight increased—he saw Tinker suddenly stagger as the table shifted—then move away from him and jump towards the attic wall, landing with a thump on the floor beneath. He looked again towards the group of people—and they were close now, just a metre away—and Frank and Kip were grinning and Lady Grant, still clutching her precious shoe, had tears running down her face and William and Kitty and Prudence were jumping up and down and hugging each other, which was a bad idea because, what with that and all their combined (and rapidly increasing) weights, the trestles supporting the great table top suddenly gave way and the whole vast expanse of plywood pancaked down to the floor with a great dusty crash.

It was lucky that Tinker was so agile. He had been sniffing around under the table at some tiny fragments of sawdust—some of which smelt like the smelly boy, some of which smelt like the little girl, and all of which smelt like those metal things in the men's tool bags—and he'd heard a creaking sound over his head and had looked up just in time to see the plywood sheets sagging down towards him. He'd jumped out of the way just as the table top smashed down—down onto the very spot where he'd been standing. And now, after all that excitement, there was the smelly boy, sitting in the ruins of the train set, looking a bit dazed but otherwise fine, so Tinker trotted up and gave him a quick lick (partly out of friendship but mostly because he tasted quite good)—and there, also sitting in a pile of wrecked, miniature houses, was his dear old lady, rubbing her hip with one hand and picking bits of plaster out of her hair with the other—and she deserved a lick too—as did all the other people, all of whom seemed a little dazed and confused; but that was all right, because the surroundings had certainly changed dramatically and, as far as Tinker was concerned, certainly for the better.

Measle began to crawl through the wreckage towards the group—but something seemed to be in his way. A rectangular block of stone, which hadn't been there a moment before, was suddenly blocking his view. He stood up, his feet crushing the entire logging camp, and began to walk round the block—but the block was getting bigger, expanding in all directions, left, right, and upwards

—and Measle looked up and saw that it was the statue from the town square. Already, the figure of the man and the woman were high above his head, just as they had been when both he and the statue had been tiny. He looked around, to see if anything else from the train set was growing—but, no. It was just the statue on its stone base, rearing up now towards the rafters.

And then there was an ominous creaking of straining floorboards.

On the other side of the statue, Kip was scrambling to his feet. He hauled Prudence up onto hers and shouted, 'Quick, everybody! The floor won't take the weight! We've got to get out of here!'

Measle met them all at the attic door. 'What's happening?' he shouted, over the creaking sound of protesting timbers.

'I don't know!' yelled Kip. 'But I do know wood—and this floor is going to give way any second now! Come on, everybody! Down the stairs and out of this house!'

They ran, stumbling down the stairs. Tinker was everywhere—under their feet, in front one minute, behind the next, barking with excitement. Down, down they went—first to the top landing, then down the main stairs—one flight, another flight—and all the time they could hear the attic floor groaning with the enormous weight that was resting on it. As they reached the hall at the foot of the stairs, a piece of plaster from the ceiling high above them crashed to the floor, shattering over the filthy carpet.

'Out! Everybody out!' screamed Kip.

Frank wrenched open the front door and they all piled out of the house and into the road, with Tinker dancing among them. When they had reached the relative safety of the opposite pavement, they all turned and looked back towards the house. For a moment, everything appeared to be normal—or as normal as the grim house could ever look, with its soot-encrusted walls and its tall, finger-like chimneys and its black-painted windows—and then, with a thunderous crash, the attic floor gave way and the great stone block, with the two statues on the top, began to fall through the house. It hit the floor beneath the attic with the sound of a bomb going off. That floor gave way instantly and the block continued on its way—smashing through the floor below, then on through the floor below that, finally ripping its way down to the street level, where it landed on the filthy carpet with an earsplitting *thump*.

And then the grim house did a very odd thing. It *sighed*. They could all hear it clearly—a great, sad exhalation of breath, as if it had lost the will to go on standing.

The chimneys were the first to go. Slowly, one toppled, then another and then another, their sooty bricks crashing through the black slate roof. The roof shuddered—and then collapsed inwards and downwards, ripping its way through what was left of the floors. The walls were last. Slowly at first, they started to crumple, falling in on themselves with increasing speed until, with a roar, the whole building disappeared in a great cloud of black dust.

The dust blew over them. It smelt of dead fish, old mattresses, and the insides of ancient sneakers. Everybody held their noses until the dust cloud settled—everybody except Tinker, who couldn't hold his nose and—even if he'd been able to—wouldn't. To Tinker, there were no really bad smells. Just *interesting* ones.

Where the house had stood was a huge pile of black rubble. In the middle of the rubble stood the statue. The stone base was buried in the fallen bricks and roof slates, but the two figures of the man and the woman stood clear above the wreckage.

Measle, his throat dry from the dust, croaked, 'What happened?'

William began to say, 'Beats me,' but he only got as far as 'Beats—' before Kip suddenly grabbed his arm and pointed at the statue. The outer stone on the two figures was beginning to crack like an eggshell. A large chunk fell off the man's head, followed by another from the woman's outstretched arms. More and more cracks appeared on the figures and more and more of the stone covering fell away—revealing to everybody's astonished eyes, the shapes of a *real* man and a *real* woman underneath. Suddenly, the man shook himself and the last of the stone fell away from his body. He reached down and began picking the remaining pieces from the woman's body, until both were free. Then he held out his hand and the woman took it. He lifted her from her knees and they clung to each other for a moment. Then they both turned and looked towards the group of people on the other side of the street.

They smiled. The man, still holding tight to the woman's hand, stepped down onto the rubble and together they picked their way over the ruins and walked across the road. When they reached the group, they stood first in front of Frank. The man let go of the woman's hand and took Frank's instead. He shook it and said, 'Thank you.' The woman reached up and kissed Frank on the cheek and she said, 'Thank you', too.

They went to each person in turn, the man shaking hands, the woman kissing cheeks. When they got to Tinker, the man fondled the dog's ears and the woman knelt down and hugged him hard, pressing her lips against his rough muzzle.

They left Measle to the last.

He looked up at the man and the woman, who were standing quietly in front of him. There was something about them both—something he could almost, but not quite, put his finger on. They looked familiar in some way, as if he'd known them both a very long time ago. Old friends, perhaps, from a distant past. Very *good* old friends. The man was tall, with curly brown hair. His eyes were brown and they wrinkled at the corners when he smiled—and they were wrinkling now. The woman was slim, her reddish hair tumbling over her shoulders. Her eyes were green, with tiny flecks of gold in them. She was, Measle decided, very pretty. She was smiling too. Measle stuck out his hand.

'Hi,' he croaked. 'I'm Measle Stubbs.'

'No, you're not,' said the man. 'Your name isn't Measle Stubbs. It's Sam Lee Stubbs. I'm your dad and I should know.'

'And I'm your mum,' said the woman and Measle looked at her and saw that, even though she was smiling as broadly as the man, she was crying. She wiped her hand across her eyes, sniffed, and said, 'And you need a *bath*.'

There were questions and explanations—and more questions and more answers—and a lot of hugging and kissing and Measle found himself unable to say anything very much because his heart was thumping in his chest and he felt like crying, although he didn't know why. He just stood and stared and grinned at the man who was his father and the woman who was his mother and, between answers and explanations, his father and his mother stood and stared and grinned at him. At last, in a pause in the babble, he tugged at the man's sleeve and said, 'Sam Lee?'

'That's your name,' said Mr Stubbs. 'The name we gave you when you were born. It's a mixture of

our names—your mother's and mine. I'm Sam
Stubbs. Mum's name is Elizabeth but everybody
calls her Lee. The wrathmonk called you "Measle"
because wrathmonks like to muddle things up. He
used all the same letters as "Sam" and "Lee", but he
mixed them around and came up with "Measle". It
was one of his many ways of trying to make you
feel bad.'

Measle thought for a moment. Then he said,
'Well, it didn't work. I don't mind Measle. I've sort
of got used to it.'

'Hey,' said Sam Stubbs, 'if you like being called
"Measle", then we'll call you "Measle".'

'Thank you very much,' said Measle. Something
funny was happening to his eyes—they seemed to
be watering quite badly—and he blinked hard to
make the wetness go away. To change the subject
(and because he really wanted to know) he said,
'Basil told me that you were killed by a deadly
snake—and that wasn't true, was it?'

Sam Stubbs raised one eyebrow. 'You don't think
so?' he said, a small smile turning up the corners of
his mouth.

'Well, Basil never lied,' said Measle. 'At least, not
as far as I know.'

Sam Stubbs nodded. 'No, he never did. And he
didn't lie about what happened to us, either. Of
course, there were a few things he left out of the
story. Things like the snake just happened to
belong to *him*. And far from being alive, it was

very, very *dead*. And it wasn't even a complete snake—just an ancient, mummified snake's head. An ancient mummified snake's head that had once wriggled about on Medusa's skull—'

'Who?' said Measle.

'Medusa. The Gorgon. Never heard of her?'

Measle shook his head. Sam Stubbs turned to Lee Stubbs and muttered, 'Not just a bath, dear. Also an *education*.' He turned back to Measle and grinned. 'Well, son—Medusa was a very nasty monster who lived thousands of years ago. She was reasonably normal-looking—as far as monsters go—except for the fact that instead of hair, she had a whole lot of horrible snakes writhing about on her head. I don't know how she ever got any sleep with all that wriggling and hissing. Anyway, if you just *looked* at Medusa, you turned to stone. One peep at her ghastly face and bang!—you're granite. Anyway, to cut a long story a bit shorter—'

'Oh, please don't,' said Measle, who was rather enjoying the tale.

'Well, I'll give you the full version later. The important part is that Basil had somehow got hold of one of her mummified snakes' heads—as you can imagine, they're pretty rare objects these days—and that's what he used on us, you see. Even dead and mummified and not even part of Medusa's scalp any more, it still had a bit of power left. Not enough to petrify us all the way through, but just enough to give us a good thick covering of stone and all before we could say, "What's that you've got in your hand, Basil?" So you see, he was sort of telling the truth all the time.'

Measle wanted to hear a lot more about Gorgons and snakes and being turned to stone—but Mrs Stubbs suddenly looked up at the sky and said, 'It's getting late, dear. I do think we ought to be getting home.'

'Home?' said Measle, hopefully.

'Home,' said Sam Stubbs. 'It's a nice big house, out in the country. Lots of land. A couple of streams, a little lake. It should still be there. I mean, only houses like this one fall over just like that. Why don't we go and see?'

Mrs Stubbs had started to stroke Measle's head. Measle found that he rather liked his head being stroked. She bent down to him and said, 'Come on, Measle. Why don't we *all* go and see?'

'OK,' said Measle, wondering if anybody else could hear the thumping of his heart.

Sam Stubbs turned to the rest of the group. 'You all of you lost a lot in there. A few years out of your lives, for a start. I'd like to help you out, if you'll let me. In the meantime, a few days of rest and relaxation won't do any of you any harm. So, I want you all to come and stay with us for a while. There's plenty of room and you'll stay as long as you like—until you get back on your feet.'

Lady Grant limped forward, holding her remaining shoe tight against her chest. 'Speaking of feet—this is so kind of you, Mr Stubbs. Unfortunately, as you can see, I've lost one of my precious Manolos—it's somewhere underneath all that *revolting* rubble—so I won't be able to walk very far—'

Sam Stubbs smiled. 'Well, we shall have to do something about that, won't we? Just a moment.'

He turned away and took a couple of steps along the pavement, separating himself from the group. He seemed to be thinking for a moment, his forehead creased in a small frown—then his face cleared and he smiled to himself. 'Funny how quickly things come back to you,' he muttered. He raised his head, closed his eyes and said, quite softly, '*Cathalme stribenrallo Manolo carfax.*'

'*What* did he say?' said William.

A small, delighted scream from Lady Grant made everybody's heads swivel in her direction. Lady Grant, still clutching her right shoe, was staring down at her feet. Both were still bare—but right beside the big toe on her left foot stood a battered and dusty, left foot, high-heeled black shoe.

Sam Stubbs grinned at her and said, 'A bit bashed about, I'm afraid—but at least no longer buried.'

'Oh dear,' said Prudence, in a nervous voice. 'Oh dear, oh dear, oh dear. Come along, everybody, I think we ought to go now. *Right* now, in fact.'

Lee Stubbs smiled round at the group. 'It's all right,' she said. 'He was just doing a little magic.'

Prudence smiled weakly. 'That's what I'm afraid of, Mrs Stubbs. I mean to say—with all due respect —what exactly is your husband?'

'He's a wizard, Miss Peyser. That was half the trouble, you see.'

'Half the trouble?'

'As far as Basil Tramplebone was concerned. But that's another story. Don't worry. My husband is a very minor wizard.'

'Oh dear. But surely you'd rather keep that a secret? I mean, we . . . um . . . we ordinary mortals aren't really supposed to know he's a wizard— isn't that so, Mrs Stubbs?'

'Well,' said Lee Stubbs, confidentially, 'I think it's probably best that you do know. After all, you've been through so much, all of you. You've known a *wrathmonk*, for goodness' sake. What's a minor wizard after that? And he's very nice, honestly he is. He wouldn't hurt a fly—unless of course . . . ' (and here Lee Stubbs lowered her voice to a whisper) '. . . unless of course the fly happened to be a *wrathmonk*.'

Lee Stubbs smiled a little, secretive sort of smile at Prudence. It was the kind of smile that said, *You know what I'm talking about, don't you?* Then she looked around and frowned in disgust.

'And now, do let's get away from this horrible place as quickly as we possibly can.'

Nobody said no, which was hardly surprising. The only remark spoken at all during the next few moments was by Prudence Peyser. She whispered into Lady Grant's ear. '*Minor* wizard indeed! I don't think so, Lady Grant. Rather *major*, I would say.'

'Really?' said Lady Grant, beaming with the prospect of mixing with members of the mystical elite. She detached herself from Prudence, put on her most winning smile, and made a beeline for Mr and Mrs Stubbs. But before she could say a single flattering thing to them, Lee Stubbs had taken one of Measle's hands and Sam Stubbs had taken the other and the three of them led the small group down and out of the dismal street for ever.

When everybody had gone and the street was once again deserted, the small black cloud floated over the rubble, looking for something to rain on. Off to one side, at the edge of the ruined house, were two patches of green slime—one very small, the other quite large. There was something about those two patches of green slime that felt right to the small black cloud, so it positioned itself directly above them and began to release its rain.

The rain fell heavily and, quite soon, the two patches of slime began to dissolve, mixing with the black dust and the water into a soupy puddle. Soon, the puddle slid into the gutter at the side of the road, slipped silently down a slight slope, and, meeting a drain set into the channel, gurgled down into the darkness of the sewers.

And the small black cloud squeezed the very last of the water out of itself and then, with nothing left to rain on, popped—with the sound of a cork being pulled from a bottle—out of existence.

Ian Ogilvy is best known as an actor—in particular for his takeover of the role of The Saint from Roger Moore. He has appeared in countless television productions, both here and in the United States, has made a number of films, and starred often on the West End stage. He has written two novels: *Loose Chippings* and *The Polkerton Giant*, both published by Headline. His play, *A Slight Hangover*, is published by Samuel French. He lives in Southern California with his wife Kitty and two stepsons.

Measle Stubbs is best known as an orphan—in particular for his unfortunate role as the charge of evil wrathmonk, Basil Tramplebone. *Measle and the Wrathmonk* is Measle's first appearance, but look out for him in *Measle and the Dragodon*, *Measle and the Mallockee*, and, coming soon, *Measle and the Slitherghoul*. Having left the house of Tramplebone, Measle is now living happily ever after (well, for the moment at least).

How about another **Measle** treat?

A small boy,
an even smaller dog, and the
biggest monster ever . . .

MEASLE AND THE DRAGODON

IAN OGILVY

Things are looking up for Measle. He's been
reunited with his parents and they're making up
for lost time and having lots of fun.
It seems too good to last.

And it is. The mysterious Dragodon and his gang
of wicked Wrathmonks have cast a spell on Measle's dad
and snatched his mum. Measle and his dog, Tinker,
have only one clue, and it leads them to the deserted
theme park—The Isle of Smiles.

Being hunted down by horrors in a dark, wet
funfair is anything but fun! Measle is on a mission
with more ups and downs than any rollercoaster—
can he save the day once again?

There's more **MEASLE** adventure in store with:

Measle's on his own again. Some double-crossing wizards have locked up his mum and dad and now they're after Measle.

He's got his baby sister with him—a baby sister with amazing magical powers—and every warlock in the place wants to get his hands on her.

Measle has to hide, and Caltrop Castle seems safe. But there's something strange about it. The creepy castle can keep the wizards and warlocks out... but what is locked inside with Measle and the mallockee...?